Falling for Texas

Jill Lynn

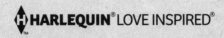

HARLEQUIN® LOVE INSPIRED®

Recycling programs
for this product may
not exist in your area.

♦TM LOVE INSPIRED BOOKS

ISBN-13: 978-0-373-81821-1

Falling for Texas

www.Harlequin.com

Printed in U.S.A.

"You have to help me with my sister," Cash said.

Olivia had already agreed to tutor Rachel. What more did the man need?

"I don't have a clue how to help her," he added. "How to deal with a teenage girl, and you have all of this experience. You'd be perfect."

Perfect was not the word that came to Olivia's mind.

"It would be so great if you could give me advice. I'm desperate to figure out how to help Rachel out of this rebellious stage she's in."

Cash flashed a charming smile, and Olivia's resolve weakened.

"I'm not sure what kind of help I would be. It's not like I have a counseling degree or anything."

"It doesn't matter. You are a woman." He cleared his throat, looking at the trail in front of them before glancing back to her. "If tonight's any indication, I obviously need help with her." Cash punctuated the quiet statement with a shake of his head, then grew silent, leaving Olivia to her own thoughts.

She needed to say no. She didn't need to add another thing that forced her into spending time with Cash. Plus, the thought of helping Cash with Rachel only reminded Olivia of her own mistakes.

But how *could* she say no?

Jill Lynn is a member of the American Christian Fiction Writers group and won the ACFW Genesis award in 2013. She has a bachelor's degree in communications from Bethel University. A native of Minnesota, Jill now lives in Colorado with her husband and two children. She's an avid reader of happily-ever-afters and a fan of grace, laughter and thrift stores. Connect with her at jill-lynn.com.

Books by Jill Lynn

Love Inspired

Falling for Texas

"For I know the plans I have for you," declares the LORD, "plans to prosper you and not to harm you, plans to give you hope and a future."
—*Jeremiah* 29:11

To my mom—thank you for always being my biggest supporter, a wise counselor and a tenacious prayer warrior.

Chapter One

His sister's skill for getting into trouble would be impressive if it weren't so discouraging.

Cash Maddox's abused leather cowboy boots echoed down the empty school hallway, the smells of industrial cleaner and mildew transporting him back a decade to his own high school days. At least the scents were better than manure, the cologne he most likely boasted after taking off in the middle of ranch work and not leaving enough time for a shower.

Usually he didn't get called into school until a few weeks into the fall semester. But this year? School hadn't even started. Rachel had only been on school property for one day of preseason volleyball practice yesterday, yet Cash had come in last night to find a note scrawled in his housekeeper's handwriting about meeting the new coach after practice today.

He didn't know what Coach Grayson wanted to meet with him about, but if he had to guess, his sister wasn't going to be winning any awards. Unless there was a gold medal for eye rolling or hair tossing. She'd win those faster than an amateur could get bucked off a bull.

But despite the tension that had invaded their house lately and the way Rachel wanted nothing to do with him, Cash loved his little sister. He'd do just about anything to give her the same great upbringing he'd had. He owed her at least that much.

Catching his reflection in the glass trophy case, Cash paused to pick out a much younger version of himself in the old football team photos. He and his best friend, Jack Smith, had that stoic look in the picture, as if smiling meant they weren't tough.

He shook his head and started walking again, remembering parading down these same hallways. Man, he'd been full of himself back then. Not more than any other football player in this town, but still. At least he and Jack had finally grown up. Cash's maturing had come a bit quicker than most, but then, parenting would do that to anyone.

He paused in the doorway to the French room, where his message said to meet.

"You must be Rachel's father. Please come in." Coach Grayson waved, not looking up from working at her desk. "I'm just finishing up some class notes."

Cash opened his mouth to correct her assumption, then clamped his jaw shut at her look of concentration. Warm cocoa hair scooped into a ponytail hung down over one shoulder as Coach Grayson nibbled on her lip.

Jack. Cash wanted to grab an old-fashioned branding iron and lay one on his friend. Jack and Janie Smith were neighbors with the new woman in town, and they'd had her over for dinner on Sunday night. But while Jack had mentioned that his wife and two-year-old son had seemed equally smitten with the new coach, he'd failed to mention that she looked nothing like Coach Pleater—the woman in her sixties who'd retired last year after two decades with the school.

Coach Grayson wore a fitted pink T-shirt and had tiny stud earrings in her earlobes. Athletic and yet still…professional. Right. That was the word he was going for.

Cash settled his long frame into the high school desk across from her and released a pent-up breath. Didn't matter if the woman was the Gillespie County Fair queen. She was off-limits for him.

He removed his hat, scraping a hand through his hair and causing a cloud of dust to settle on his shoulders. Yep. Definitely should have showered.

"Sorry about that. I didn't want to lose that thought for the first week's lesson plan." Coach Grayson set her pen down and looked up, gracing Cash with breath-stealing blue eyes framed by dark lashes and plenty of reasons to escape from the room right now. Like a heart-shaped face, with a chin that jutted out just enough to emphasize the smooth curve of her cheeks and the line of her lips.

Mercy. What was wrong with him? Had he never seen a woman before?

"No problem." At his raspy voice, he cleared his throat and tried again. "You wanted to see me about Rachel?"

Coach Grayson's eyebrows pulled together and she looked down at the front of her shirt—searching for words or embarrassed about her clothing, Cash wasn't sure. He only knew the coach didn't look anywhere near as messy in her volleyball gear as he did in grubby ranch clothes. In fact, she looked pretty cute.

Not that he should be looking.

Cash forced his concentration back to his sister instead of the surprising distraction in front of him. After all, he had a promise to keep and a girl who needed him to keep it.

The rest would have to wait.

So far, Olivia Grayson considered her escape from Colorado a success. In one weekend, she'd managed to move across the country, unpack her apartment, become friends with her new neighbors and fall in love.

If that last one happened to be with Jack and Janie Smith's two-year-old son? All the better. Olivia had no intention of meeting a guy in the sleepy little town of Fredericksburg, Texas.

Which was why she absolutely *did not care* that a head-turning cowboy sat across from her while she wore a coffee-stained T-shirt boasting the lovely smell of a productive day in the gym.

Olivia hadn't thought much of it when she'd pictured meeting Rachel Maddox's father. But if the man in front of her was a parent to the seventeen-year-old blonde on her volleyball team, Olivia would swallow her tongue.

She kind of already had.

"You're Warren Maddox?"

"Actually, I'm Cash." He ran a hand through dark hazelnut hair speckled with a few sun-kissed golden highlights. "Warren's my father's name. Technically I'm Warren C. Maddox, but everyone's called me Cash since I was a kid. Warren is probably listed as my legal name on the parent list. Sorry about that."

Olivia waited for some further explanation, but it didn't come. Huh. Maybe he'd had Rachel at a very young age. Or something.

Was it really her business?

"So, what's my sister done this time?"

"Your sister?"

He nodded. "Suppose you wouldn't know the

story, being new and all. Rachel is my younger sister by ten years. Our parents died in a car crash a few years ago and I was old enough to take legal guardianship of her."

That made a lot more sense. Except...what a horrible story. "I'm so sorry." Olivia straightened the stack of papers on her desk, floundering for more appropriate words to express her sympathies. She quickly discarded everything that popped into her mind.

Cash raised a hand. "You don't have to stop talking to me now or analyze everything you say before you say it."

She smiled as his mesmerizing hazel eyes turned playful, the color reminding her of leaves changing in the fall.

"I can't believe you thought I was old enough to be Rachel's father, Coach Grayson. Now that's just offensive."

"I didn't think that."

Her gaze traveled from his T-shirt that sported evidence of a hard day's work, down to his dusty jeans and brown leather boots. The way his legs covered the distance between his chair and her desk, he must be over six foot. Which meant he was taller than her...not that that mattered in the least.

He skimmed a hand over strong cheekbones. "I

apologize for my appearance, but I had to come in the middle of ranch work to meet with you."

Had he noticed her perusal? Heat rushed to her cheeks. Dust might permeate the man's appearance, but he definitely didn't need to apologize. He looked far too attractive for his disheveled state.

"I'm sorry for pulling you away from work." She glanced down at her clothes. "And I just came from practice, so I completely understand." Olivia swiped her mouth to check for the presence of any chocolate left from her after-practice snack. With the way she was acting, she'd probably find a bit of drool, too.

"It's not a problem, Coach Grayson. Rachel always comes first."

"Call me Olivia, please." If Rachel came first… did that mean Cash wasn't married? He had to be around her age. "Was that your wife that I spoke to on the phone to schedule our meeting?"

An amused grin slid across his face, making Olivia's stomach bounce like one of the volleyballs she'd put away after practice.

"I ask Laura Lee to marry me all the time, but she always says no. Probably because she's already married to my foreman, Frank." His eyes danced. "Laura Lee helps out at the house. She's really more of an aunt or a mother than a housekeeper. She works a few hours a week cleaning and making meals. Freezes a bunch at a time so we have something to eat. If Rachel or I were in charge of meals, it would only be fast food or frozen pizzas."

Olivia let out a breath she didn't realize she'd been holding. Of relief? Did it really matter if he was married or not? She didn't have plans to go anywhere near another man. Not after the mess she'd left behind in Colorado.

She glanced down, the papers on her desk bringing the reason for their meeting back into focus. "Now that I've figured out who you are, I guess we should talk about Rachel." That came out sounding so professional she almost cheered.

Cash leaned back, linking fingers behind his neck and crossing one leg over the other. "I am curious what Rachel did to warrant a meeting this time. Usually it's a few weeks into school before I get the first phone call."

The girl sounded like a bit of trouble. Good thing Olivia had a soft spot for struggling teenage girls. Hoping Cash wouldn't get too upset about what she had to say next, she leaned forward and softened her voice. "She didn't do anything wrong. Yet."

When Cash mirrored her smile, Olivia ignored the way her disobedient legs swam under the desk.

"I've been going over last year's grades, and I'm concerned that if Rachel doesn't make some changes this year she won't be eligible to play due to her GPA. I don't know if you realize this, but your sister's very good."

She paused, wondering how much to share with him. The man probably needed some encouragement if he had to deal with a teenage girl all on his own. "In two days of practice I can tell she's the best player I've ever coached. And if you think I look too young for that to matter, you're wrong. I have enough experience to know what I'm saying. She definitely has the potential to play in college and could easily earn a scholarship. I'd hate to see her lose out on that because of her GPA."

A line cut through Cash's forehead, and Olivia pressed her lips together. Had she pushed too far?

"I'm not sure what to do with that girl. Ever since our parents died she's had trouble, but never to this degree. I try to talk to her, but she won't open up to me. It seems her grades and behavior keep getting worse instead of better."

"What about a tutor or someone to help her complete her class assignments during the school year? I looked up her test scores and I'm pretty sure from what I saw that she's just not applying herself. The scores show she's smart, which makes me think she doesn't care enough to do the work her classes require."

Cash let out an exhale that turned into a laugh as he shook his head. "That sounds like my sister." His arms slid around the cowboy hat on the desk as he shifted forward.

Sensing openness, Olivia's tense muscles relaxed. If only all parents were so receptive.

"Have any free time on your hands, Coach Grayson? Any chance you'd be interested in tutoring one of your new players?"

That was not what Olivia had expected to hear. A small part of her found the idea intriguing. In practice, she could see the hurt hiding behind Rachel's eye rolls and teenage attitude. But Olivia didn't need to get involved with this family. Not when the man across from her had a melt-her-resolve grin that could get her into serious trouble. Again.

"I…might be able to work something out." She wanted to jump out of her chair, grab the words and stuff them back into her mouth. Why would she offer to help Rachel? She absolutely did not have the time. And she needed to stay far, far away from the magnetic Cash Maddox.

"I'd be happy to pay you for your time."

Did he sense her reluctance? "I can't accept payment for tutoring one of the students. It's against the rules and I wouldn't take it anyway."

Olivia frowned. *Quit making it sound like you're still considering it. Open your mouth right now and tell him you can't do it.*

"Volleyball has games on Wednesday nights, right?" Cash barely waited for her nod before continuing. "How about Thursdays after practice you come out to the ranch and help Rachel? We'll pay you by feeding you dinner. Don't worry, I won't make it myself. I'll warm up whatever Laura Lee has in the freezer."

Take back your semioffer and say no.

But…

What if digging up twenty-six years of roots in Colorado and roaring into this Texas town with a trail of dirt behind her wasn't just about running away from her past? What if God had brought her here to help a young girl?

For such a time as this… The verse she'd read in Esther last night pounded through her head and Olivia sighed, resisting the urge to close her eyes or crawl under the desk to escape. "Guess I could swing that."

"Great." Cash's eyebrows shot up as if her answer surprised him. Kind of like it had her. He extracted himself from the desk and she found out the truth to her theory. Definitely taller than her.

"I'll see you the first week of school, then. I hope you know how much we appreciate this." Cash returned the cowboy hat to his head, tipped the brim in her direction and exited the room, leaving Olivia wondering about the state of her decision-making skills.

What had she been thinking agreeing to help? Better yet, what was God thinking?

If anything, God should want to keep her far

away from Cash Maddox. Five minutes with the man and Olivia already felt a tug of attraction—to Cash's personality, not just his looks. But she would just have to bury any thoughts of him under her spinning tires. Moving to Texas was all about starting over and leaving the past behind…which meant no dating, no more mistakes.

She might have arrived in Fredericksburg with memories clinging to the trunk of her car and an empty ring finger stripped of all hope, but she refused to repeat the past here.

No looking back. It could be her Texas motto.

The open-air Jeep Wrangler jerked and dipped as Cash drove toward the new pasture site, hands rumbling on the steering wheel. His meeting with Coach Grayson—Olivia—had eaten enough time out of the afternoon that the guys most likely had the portable electric fences in place.

He shoved the stick shift into first gear, pulled on the parking brake and turned off the engine. Leaving the keys dangling in the ignition, he jumped out.

"How we doing?" Cash approached Frank, adjusting the brim of his hat to better shade against the sizzling mid-August sun.

"Just about ready to move them over." Frank studied the grazing cattle, his face weathered from a lifetime of outdoor work. He'd been the foreman at the Circle M for as long as Cash could remember. Frank didn't say much, but when he did, that usually meant it needed to be said. He had a wise, level head on his shoulders and had helped Cash keep the ranch running after Dad died. Frank knew more about ranching than twenty experienced ranch hands roped together.

A wet snout nosed his hand and Cash looked down into Cocoa's happy face. "Ready to move some cattle, girl?" The Australian cattle dog gave a happy bark, head nodding in agreement. She was as much of an institution around the Circle M as Frank. Mouth painted in a permanent smile, Cocoa looked up at him as if to say, *What are we waiting for?* Cash laughed at the dog's silly grin and leaned down to rub her head. Her eyes squinted shut as if she was enjoying a fancy massage, tongue lolling out the side of her mouth. "Hang on a minute. We're almost there." At Cash's words, Cocoa settled into the grass, laying her black head and contrasting white snout on her tan paws with a pout.

Cash headed for the water trough connected to wells by pipelines that spanned the ranch. While he waited for the trough to fill, he took off his hat and swiped his brow with the back of his arm. Frustration over Rachel's grades boiled up as quickly as the afternoon heat. He knew she wasn't applying herself—knew she had it in her to do better. But he didn't know how to make her. Losing their parents had shaken her to the core. She'd struggled in the four years since their deaths, but lately her attitude and grades seemed even worse.

Blake Renner probably had something to do with that, though Cash had yet to convince his sister that the boy did not have her best interests at heart.

Frank took a wide stance next to Cash, the sun squinting off his larger-than-life belt buckle as Rants and Noble hopped in the ranch truck with a wave, heading back to the barn. The ancient vehicle boasted an impressive oil leak, but it still managed to function for any work that needed to be done on the ranch.

"Sorry I had to take off before we were done."

"No problem. Rachel comes first." Frank's brow crinkled with concern. "Everything okay?"

"Yeah." If he didn't count his sister's failing grades or the volleyball coach he should be avoiding who would be spending Thursday nights at the ranch. "Rach needs to get her grades up to stay on the team."

A slow nod proved Frank had heard. "She'll be all right. Reckon she's had a tough time of it the last few years."

That was an understatement that made Cash's inadequacies as a guardian rear up.

"You're doing the best you can." Frank whacked Cash on the back. "Enough of that now. Let's get the horses and move these cattle."

Hours later, Cash strode from the barn in time to see Rachel's Wrangler bumping into the yard with typical teenage flair, somehow landing in her parking spot. The vehicle abuse made him wince, though he'd be more concerned about her relaxed habits if he hadn't taught her to drive himself.

Dinner would have to be sandwiches tonight. They'd worked too late for him to defrost anything. But at least his little sister had decided to show up. He had to look for the silver lining with her.

The sun touched the trees to the west, setting the green leaves aflame with gold and orange. Cash tipped his head back, stealing a moment of peace before the storm.

After a deep breath, he headed for Rachel, knowing he needed to tell her about Coach Grayson offering to tutor her. He almost laughed out loud. *Offering* might not be the right word. He'd sensed that Olivia had planned to say no. But then he'd pushed a little harder, hoping she'd give in. Was it for his sister's benefit or his own? He didn't want to think about the answer to that question.

What would his parents have done in this situation? As usual, the thought left Cash feeling ill equipped. In the moment, asking Olivia to help had seemed like the best option. But now the thought of spending time around the coach gave him a bit of panic.

He squared his shoulders. He'd just have to keep

any attraction he felt tucked away where no one could see it. Surely he could handle Thursday nights without going back on his promise.

Rachel hopped down from the Wrangler and reached back in to grab her bag. She turned, greeting him with a defiant toss of her ponytail, and he cringed. Like taming a wild mustang.

Somehow, he needed to get through to her. Make her understand that she'd get kicked off the team if her grades didn't improve.

No matter the reason, he knew one thing for sure. She was *not* going to like it.

Chapter Two

"You agreed to *what*?" Janie Smith's voice came out as a high-pitched squeak, reminding Olivia of the few months in junior high she'd attempted the clarinet.

So much for the relaxation of a pedicure.

"I'm a little shocked myself." Olivia shifted her feet in the hot, bubbling water, took a sip of her blended mocha and tried to get back to a place of calm. Saturday morning girl time with Janie was *supposed* to be the perfect ending to her first week of all-day practices. And after the stress of yesterday's final team cuts—never an easy decision—she desperately needed some relaxation. Olivia was still praying for the girls she'd had to move to the JV team.

Janie rubbed her hands together, copper eyes sparkling. "I think someone has a little crush on you and wants you around." The massage elements rotated up and down behind her as she did a dance in the oversized chair, sandy-brown hair swinging around her chin.

"Ha. He offered to pay me. I don't think that constitutes a crush." Olivia turned to better face the woman who already felt like an old friend even though they'd only met eight days ago. "I can see the wheels turning in your head, and you need to let that idea go. He finagled me into helping a struggling high school girl get her grades up—one of my best players, too. No harm in that."

Janie's face perked with interest. "Did you know he's Jack's best friend? You two would be perfect for each other!"

The smell of high-voltage perm wafted over Olivia as the woman on her right leaned closer, tight curls covering her head like bright red caterpillars. She pursed coral-colored lips as she pretended to read a magazine.

"Did you hear anything I just said?" Olivia lowered her voice, leaning closer to Janie. "This is exactly why I should have said no in the first place. Not only are you jumping to conclusions, pretty soon the whole town will be talking about it." She scooted back, letting the *thump-thump-thump* of the massage chair chisel into the tension radiating through her shoulders.

"Okay, okay. I'll let it go." Janie raised an unmanicured hand in defeat. Being a nurse, Janie had agreed with Olivia and opted out of getting her nails done. Both used their hands too much in their jobs for the polish to stay on longer than a day or two without chipping.

"For now." Janie added the last part under her breath as she picked up a magazine, smirk in place.

Olivia went back to perusing the latest fashions in hers. The smell of sample perfumes leaked from the pages, fighting off the chemical smell from the fake nails being done across the room.

She toyed with the tips of her mocha hair, wondering if she should add a new cut or color to her new life. After the shattering of her heart a year ago, she'd done a makeover and ended up with longer layers. She'd kept the style because she liked it and felt as if it softened her face—not because she still had something to prove.

"Just so you know, he hasn't dated anyone in years."

Olivia glanced at the black-and-white clock on the wall with amusement. For three and a half glorious minutes, Janie had managed to stay quiet on the subject of Cash.

"And it's not from a lack of women trying, either. Good-looking. Owns a ranch. Took custody of his little sister. What's not to want?" Janie peeked out from behind her magazine shield.

"He only asked me to tutor his sister. He did not ask me out." Olivia ignored the disappointment that crawled up her spine. She could not, would not, have any interest in Cash. And now she sounded like a Dr. Seuss book. But she felt certain that writing a new beginning in Texas meant that one of these days, her hurt would ebb away and she'd be able to move forward. One of these days, she'd forgive herself for making the biggest mistake of her life.

Unfortunately, those new feelings didn't rush in with the pedicure water bubbling around her feet.

Janie leaned closer and Olivia felt Perm Lady do the same.

"I'm just saying that it's been a long time since he's shown interest in someone. You can think the tutoring is only for Rachel, but I wouldn't be surprised if he has ulterior motives."

Olivia shifted quickly to the right, giggling with Janie when Perm Lady readjusted her position so fast she almost fell out of her pedicure chair.

"Fine." The only way to end the conversation would be to give in—a little. "Here's my compromise. At this point it's strictly business. If anything changes you'll be the first to know." *And nothing is going to change.*

Janie flashed a smile laced with victory—as if she could read Olivia's mind and accepted the challenge. She tapped her plastic coffee cup against Olivia's. "I'll toast to that."

The young girl behind the coffee counter yawned as she took Olivia's money the next morning. *Tell me about it.* Olivia glanced at her watch. Seven a.m. on a Sunday—a day she could sleep in—and yet she'd found herself up at six. Haunted. Just like she'd been in Colorado.

She hadn't had the dream since a week before she moved. She'd hoped and prayed it wouldn't follow her to Texas, but it had. Brown curls. A little girl running. Always out of reach.

Olivia shuddered and moved to the end of the counter as the barista steamed the milk for her mocha. She was supposed to ride to church later this morning with the Smiths, but after waking early from the jarring images, she'd had to get out of her apartment.

The barista handed her a bright yellow mug and matching plate with a blueberry muffin perched on a paper doily. Olivia migrated toward the back of the coffeehouse, snatching a rumpled copy of the *Fredericksburg Standard* from an abandoned table along the way.

She settled into a comfy armchair and took a sip of her mocha, eyes closing in relief as the combination of sugar and caffeine rolled across her tongue. Olivia propped open the paper and ate her muffin, reading about the local pool being fixed, the proposal to plan an alternate truck route around Fredericksburg and the race for city council. Advertisements for the quaint bed-and-breakfasts that permeated Texas Hill Country filled the pages, along with an announcement for an upcoming German festival.

She stopped to text Janie that she'd meet them at church and then moved on to the sports section.

It already held talk about the approaching football season. Olivia perused the opinions, wondering how Jack handled all the pressure as the high school football coach. Made her thankful that Texas football would be at the forefront of everyone's minds, leaving her to manage her team with much less scrutiny.

"Excuse me."

Olivia looked up into the face of a man she didn't recognize. "Yes?"

"I'm sorry to bother you, but are you the new French teacher and volleyball coach?"

Back in Denver, no stranger would ever walk up to her like this, let alone actually know her. Olivia took a deep breath. She was still reeling from the dream. No need to take her frustrations out on the poor guy in front of her.

She said yes and introduced herself, shaking his outstretched hand.

"Gil Schmidt. I'm the counselor over at the high school."

Dressed in khaki shorts and a short-sleeved, button-down shirt, he was just the preppy type her younger—and much shorter—sister would consider attractive. But guys who towered over Lucy only came to Olivia's chin. Not that it bothered her anymore. She'd long ago accepted that she would never own a closet full of fashionable heels.

Unless she met a man like Cash—as tall as Cash, she corrected, stopping that train of thought before it got way off track.

Olivia glanced around the shop, surprised to find it had filled. "Would you like to join me?" She regretted the words the instant they came out of her mouth.

Gil checked his watch. "Thanks, but I've been here for a bit and now I'm headed over to church. Just thought I'd stop and introduce myself. I'm sure I'll be seeing more of you once school starts."

She said goodbye and waved as he walked away, kicking herself for being so judgmental. Gil seemed like a nice guy. She'd have to get used to living in a small town.

Shocked at the time, Olivia grabbed her purse, depositing her mug and plate in the bin for dirty dishes on the way up front.

Gil stood looking out the glass door at the front of the shop, watching the rain that now covered the sidewalks and street. When had it started raining? Guess she'd been lost in her own world, tucked in the back of the shop.

Cars whooshed by, splashing through puddles with a sizzling noise that made Olivia think about bacon. She probably should have had more than a muffin with her coffee.

She glanced at Gil. "Everything okay?"

He motioned outside with a wry grin. "I hadn't been expecting this. I rode my bike this morning."

"Do you need a ride? I'm going to Cedar Hills Church." They stepped to the side as a couple entered, shaking the water from their clothes.

"That's where I go, too."

"Can you put your bike in my trunk?"

When she pointed out her car, Gil laughed. "I don't think it will fit. It's not a problem, though. I'll wait it out."

"Why don't I give you a ride back after? Surely it will be done raining by then. Can you leave your bike here?"

He nodded slowly. "I don't think they'd mind. Are you sure?"

Olivia studied Gil's brown eyes, smiling in relief when she didn't see a spark of interest. "Absolutely. Let's go."

They chatted about school on the short ride to church and Olivia relaxed. She could use more friends in this town. But during the service, Gil turned attentive—holding open the Bible for them to read together, sitting just a little closer than she'd like.

Had she led him on by offering him a ride? Her no-dating rule applied to everyone in this town, not just the entirely too-attractive man sitting one row behind her with his sister.

Maybe Gil didn't mean anything by his actions. Olivia's instincts could be way off. They had been in the past.

Olivia stood for the closing song, Gil's arm pressing against hers, and the pastor closed with her favorite benediction: "The Lord bless you and keep you. The Lord make His face shine on you and be gracious to you. The Lord turn His face toward you and give you peace."

Amen.

Olivia followed Gil into the aisle, then waited for Janie. She and Jack had sat farther down in the same row.

"I'll meet you in the narthex. I need to find someone." Gil squeezed Olivia's arm, then made his way down the aisle.

She resisted the urge to rub away his touch as Janie came out of the row and latched onto her. "Gil Schmidt?"

The church emptied as Olivia explained her morning—minus the dream.

"Hmm." Janie's brow furrowed. "Guess Cash

better get his behind in gear." Her face brightened. "Might light a fire under him, knowing he's not the only admirer you have in town."

"I thought we agreed yesterday to leave things alone in that department."

"You agreed to that. Not me." Grinning like a puppy who'd demolished a shoe, Janie linked arms with Olivia and directed them to Jack and Cash, standing together in the narthex.

"Jack, we need to get Tucker." Janie slid away from Olivia and tugged on her husband's arm.

Matchmaking woman. Olivia resisted the urge to roll her eyes like she'd seen the girls on her team do more times than she could count.

Jack didn't budge. "Can you run and get him? I need to talk to Cash."

Janie's copper eyes flashed as she braced a hand on her slender hip. "Fine. I'll go myself."

"I'll go with you."

Janie greeted Olivia's offer with a wave of her hand, turning sweet as cherry pie. "No, Liv, don't worry about it. I'll be right back."

Jack watched his wife walk away until she disappeared. When a gorgeous redhead approached Cash, Jack pulled Olivia to the side. "I need to ask a favor. Our anniversary is coming up and I want to surprise Janie and take her to San Antonio for dinner. It's a drive, so it would be a late evening. Usually my parents or Janie's would be available, but they're all attending a church function that night. It's the first Saturday in September."

"And you want me to chauffeur?" Olivia laughed at the scowl on Jack's face. "I'd love to hang out with my favorite little man." *Even if it breaks my heart a little every time.*

"Thanks, I appreciate it. We owe you a dinner."

She waved off Jack's thanks. "You don't owe me a thing."

"Guess I'd better go find my wife." Jack grinned. "She's going to kill me for not leaving you here alone with Cash."

Olivia's chin dropped. So the man only pretended innocence. She shoved him on the arm, then spotted Gil across the way talking to an older gentleman.

After only a few steps in his direction, Olivia felt a warm hand wrap around her arm. Goose bumps spread in waves across her skin, leaving no doubt whom she'd turn to find. Her mind might have made a decision not to have any interest in Cash, but her body didn't seem to accept the verdict as easily.

"Coach Grayson, wait up."

She steeled herself before facing Cash. The supermodel, thankfully, was no longer attached to him. He sported a much cleaner version of the outfit he'd worn Tuesday: nice jeans, newer-looking boots—though they still had that worn, casual look—and an untucked button-down instead of a T-shirt.

"I didn't give you directions to the ranch for tutoring next week. That is, if you're still planning to start the first week of school."

Olivia snapped her attention back to his face. "I am."

Cash didn't answer right away. In fact, he didn't seem to realize she'd answered him. The man was completely distracted. Probably still thinking about the beauty he'd just been talking to.

Frustration coursed through Olivia. Could he not listen to her for two seconds? Why had he even chased her down? *Because he cares about his sister, that's why.*

Janie couldn't be more wrong in her assessment. And the sooner Olivia got her head straight, the better. Thursday nights would be about tutoring Rachel and nothing more.

How many times would she have to remind herself that's exactly what she wanted?

Cash let his gaze travel down from Olivia's flushed face, enjoying the view more than he should. He'd seen her in volleyball gear, but this was the first time he'd seen her together and styled. He wasn't sure which of the looks he liked best. Each had its own particular appeal.

Today she wore a skirt, showcasing legs as long

as Texas that tapered into strappy sandals. Her toes were painted the color of pink cotton candy and her arms—what a strange thing to be attracted to—were somehow toned and feminine at the same time.

Seeing Olivia in church this morning only made her more appealing. But watching her with Gil Schmidt? That he could do without. Gil had even held the Bible out for Olivia, as though the two of them were a couple. Who knew, maybe they were. Cash didn't have any right to get involved. Any right to care. But that didn't make it any easier to watch.

Her foot tapped while she studied him with an expectant look. Had she said something to him?

"I'm sorry, what was that you said?"

She crossed her arms. "I'm still planning on it."

"Great." That was a good thing, right? Then why did she look as though someone had broken into her apartment? Spitting mad, eyes flashing. She even tossed her hair. It fell in layers past her shoulders today instead of being up in a ponytail. Her shampoo wafted over. Something mint. She probably wouldn't appreciate it if he leaned in for closer examination.

What exactly had he done to make her so mad? Or maybe it wasn't him that had her all fired up. Maybe she didn't appreciate Gil's advances. That thought made a slow smile spread across his face.

A breath whooshed out from Olivia, filled with enough frustration to spark the room into a raging inferno.

"Where's your phone?"

He slid it from his pocket and she snatched it, her fingers flying across the keys.

"There's my number." She snapped it back into his palm and he resisted the urge to grab her hand and keep her there. "Text me directions later."

Olivia took off, leaving Cash in a strange wake of confusion. After talking to Gil for a minute, the two of them walked out the doors together. Cash rubbed his chest, wondering why it felt as if one of his longhorns had speared him. He only had enough room in his life to deal with one girl at a time. Olivia being mad at him or even dating Gil should be a good thing.

Too bad it didn't feel that way.

Chapter Three

Cash shook the thoughts of Olivia from his mind, scanning the narthex for his sister. Tera Lawton's eyes gleamed from across the room, reminding him of a jungle cat about to strike its prey. He'd already dealt with her once this morning and he didn't care to do it again.

Why couldn't the woman get the fact that he was taken? At least in one sense of the word. And even if he could date, it wouldn't be her again.

Not after what she'd done.

When Jack reappeared, Cash met his friend by the doors.

"Janie and Tucker must have already gone outside." Jack pushed out into the bright sunlight and glanced at Cash. "Trying to escape the Tera-dactyl?"

He laughed. "You know it. What is that girl thinking? As if I'd ever entertain that idea."

Jack shrugged. "She probably just wants you for your money."

Cash snorted. "You mean she's attracted to the hundred bucks in my bank account? And here I thought she couldn't resist my stunning good looks."

Jack slapped him on the back. Hard. "Must be thinking of someone else there. You never had any of those." Jack's slow drawl brought out the Texan in him, flashing Cash's mind back to their younger days. Both had grown up here, and both had returned after college. Living in Fredericksburg without Jack would be like a football game without a pigskin.

"How's the football team looking?"

"I've got a few boys hoping for scholarships, which usually means I can mold them into the kind of players I need. When they want to get out of here bad enough, they work pretty hard."

"True. But I'm not sure why anyone would want to leave this place." Cash glanced at the Texas sky, now a mixture of clouds and a striking blue color that reminded him an awful lot of a certain volleyball coach's eyes, which had just been flashing at him inside the church.

"I know what you mean."

It took Cash a minute to remember what they'd been talking about. He scanned the still-damp parking lot until he saw Janie and Tucker near

Jack's car. He must have searched too long, because Jack's laugh sounded next to him.

"She already left with Gil. Didn't you see?"

Annoying that Jack could read his mind like that. And yeah, he'd seen. Cash's hand itched to adjust the brim of a hat. Any hat that would shade a bit of his face.

"I was in church this morning, *if* you recall." Jack's amusement increased. "Probably wasn't the only one who witnessed the way you tracked her every move."

Cash winced. He had thought he'd done a better job than that of hiding his attraction to the new volleyball coach and French teacher. *French.* A sophisticated woman, who not only spoke but taught French, would surely never stay in a little town like this. Probably just passing through. Maybe he could tamp down his interest by thinking of her as a hoity-toity French teacher. Although on Tuesday she hadn't seemed too high-and-mighty. She'd seemed sweet. And this morning? Feisty. Unfortunately both of those things appealed to him.

Time for a subject change. "While you're at it, why don't you get a scholarship going for Renner? Hopefully he's got plans that don't involve this town." *Or my sister.* The star running back had a reputation for raising a ruckus, and Jack had just as little patience for him as Cash.

"Couldn't agree more. Are you coming over to watch the Rangers game this afternoon?"

They approached the car and Cash went down in time to receive the direct hit from Tucker, his little body creating a surprisingly strong tackle. "Planning on it," Cash answered Jack and then spoke to Tucker. "Has your daddy been teaching you to tackle?"

Tucker grinned, head bobbing.

"Do you want to go way up?"

At Tucker's nod, Cash hoisted the boy onto his shoulders. Tucker clapped, then settled in by squealing and gripping Cash's hair like a handlebar.

He ignored the blood rushing to his scalp as Janie looked up to greet him. The tiny woman looked like a wind might blow her over, but she handled Jack—and the whole football team—with ease. Jack hadn't figured out how amazing Janie was until college, but then he'd asked her out and never looked back.

Cash smiled at the best thing that had ever happened to his best friend. "How's my favorite girl?" He only said the phrase to annoy Jack, who promptly elbowed him in the gut.

He grunted and laughed, and Janie shook her head, the sun dancing off her cute little bob of a haircut as she ignored them both.

"Speaking of favorite girls, is Rachel coming over today, too?"

Cash shook his head, forgetting Tucker's grip and quickly regretting it. "Don't think she's planning on it." Annoyance rose up. Rachel had been spending as little time as possible in his presence. He didn't know if it was typical girl stuff or something more. Not that he knew what typical girl stuff was. He wished she'd go over to the Smiths' with him today. Janie would be good for the girl.

They said goodbyes and Cash deposited Tucker in his car seat, leaving the confusion of buckles for Jack to sort through. He headed for his dark blue extended cab truck a few spots away, got in and pressed the horn to make Tucker laugh.

That boy had stolen his heart from the first time Cash saw him in the hospital. He knew he'd done the same to Jack. Watching his friend be a father was pretty touching, but Jack and Cash didn't usually get into sappy conversations like that. The two of them didn't need to say much to know what the other was thinking. For instance, right now, Jack was probably thinking about getting in a quick nap before the Rangers game. Too bad Cash couldn't do the same.

Cash drove up to the church entrance and texted his sister. Minutes later, Rachel came out and hopped into the truck. She messed around on her phone during the fifteen-minute drive home, leaving Cash to process his day and week.

It was his turn to handle the barn today, but that shouldn't take too long. A few chores and he could grab a sandwich and head over to Jack's. But of the list of things that came to mind that he needed to accomplish during the rest of the week, only one thing really mattered. And that was keeping his concentration on his sister instead of the completely distracting volleyball coach who happened to be a Christian.

Olivia stood in the middle of the H-E-B grocery store parking lot on Saturday morning, her team spread around her. The girls had really jelled during the second week of preseason practice—a good thing, since school started on Monday and their first game was on Wednesday. But first, they had to deal with the all-important business of raising money for fall sports, starting with today's car wash.

"There's one rule. No dumping water on the coach. If you think I've already made cuts, think again."

Laughter threaded through the team.

"Come on, Coach! Mom said she'd get doused if we earn enough." Valerie Nettles's silver-braces smile widened when the rest of the team cheered in agreement with her.

Olivia turned to her assistant coach. Trish Nettles hadn't been able to take the two preseason practice weeks off from her job, so she planned to start working with the team once they began after-school practice. Bless the woman for being willing to work the Saturday morning fund-raiser, too.

At first Olivia had been concerned about having a parent as assistant coach, but Trish had assured her she'd be there to help—not control. Including her daughter's playing time. That had given Olivia peace. Truthfully, she was thankful for the help. Trish had a relationship with the girls from years past and twenty-five years' playing experience. From the conversations they'd already had about the team—and life—Olivia thought they'd get along well.

"It's true." Trish shrugged, her eyes dancing with mischief. "It's tradition. But they do need to earn a lot of money."

Olivia's lips curved up. "How much money?"

"A thousand?" At Trish's answer, the team screeched and complained, causing Trish and Olivia to share an amused look.

"A thousand it is."

Dispersing in grumbles, the girls started filling buckets with water and soap. With the sun already baking them, Olivia made sure everyone had sunscreen on, then stationed herself with a hose for rinsing. She welcomed the mist that drifted across her sizzling skin as she sprayed each car down.

Soon a line of cars snaked around the back of the parking lot. The town of Fredericksburg made supporting high school sports an art form.

Janie and Tucker rolled through, then parked after their wash and walked over. Olivia handed her job off to one of the girls and headed over to meet them near the water bottles.

"Hey, little man." Olivia's heart hiccuped when Tucker barreled into her legs. A hug or a tackle, she wasn't sure. Either way, she'd take it. She scooped Tucker up and pushed aside all of the remorse that rushed in with his sweet baby smell.

"Girl, it is hot out here. Are you dying?"

"A little." Olivia took a long swig of her water and wiped the back of her hand across her forehead. She must look a mess. "Where's Jack?"

Janie motioned to the line. "Right behind me. He drove his own car so he could get it washed too. Oh, there's Cash in his truck."

Olivia shaded her eyes, waving at Cash along with Janie. She imagined her friend's pulse didn't race as if she'd just run lines in the gym.

And you're planning to spend time with that man? Not your best move, Liv.

She hadn't seen Cash since last Sunday at church, when she'd let her initial attraction grow into a moment of jealousy. Thankfully she'd had a week to collect herself since then. Olivia had come to the realization that she couldn't avoid the man. She not only coached his sister but she also planned to tutor the girl. And Cash was friends with Jack and Janie. So Olivia had decided that she could hang out with Cash in those various settings, but she wouldn't let her heart get involved. That barely beating organ had been trampled, so keeping it tucked away until it healed only made sense.

Olivia would think of Cash as Rachel's older brother or Jack and Janie's friend and nothing more. How hard could that be?

When Jack parked and joined them, Tucker squealed. Olivia deposited him on the ground, and he toddled over to his dad. Jack snapped him up, making him giggle.

"I've noticed almost the whole football team seems to be in line." Olivia nudged Jack. "School spirit?"

He snorted. "More like girl spirit."

At the sound of screams, Olivia glanced over. One of the football players had jumped out of the passenger seat of a car and stolen a bucket of water. Girls and suds went everywhere as he doused the nearest members of her team. Two more football players emerged from their cars and Olivia groaned.

"Jack." Janie took Tucker and pushed her husband toward the chaos. "Stop them."

Before Jack could take a step, more car doors than Olivia could count opened and shut. One football player climbed out of a sunroof while the rest looked like ants swarming a lemonade spill.

Olivia ran for the hose, securing that. Jack tried yelling for them to stop, but only got himself doused with a bucketful of suds by his players. White bubbles clung to his eyebrows and nose, his look deadly.

"That's it." Jack growled and sprinted for the hose located across the car from Olivia. He opened fire and the boys ran for cover, trying to find protection from the water spray.

Janie screeched and Olivia looked behind her to see her friend's cute capris and tank top dripping with water, her formerly swaying brown bob now plastered to her head. She pointed at her husband. "Jack Edward Smith. You are a dead man."

From next to Janie's legs, Tucker clapped his hands and chanted, "Wa-wa, wa-wa."

Trish swooped in, claiming Tucker and allowing Janie to run for cover.

Using the hood for protection, Olivia ducked down. Nobody messed with her friends. She closed one eye and aimed the nozzle, then waited for the right moment. Jack's grin evaporated when the cold spray reached his stomach. He caught sight of her and she ducked, but not before a line of water shot across the top of her head.

She wasn't going down without a fight. Bracing for cold water impact, Olivia stood, aiming for Jack. But when Cash bounded around the hood of the car, she quickly switched her aim to him, hand poised on the trigger.

He stopped a foot in front of her, his grin making her stomach do crazy things. "The way I see it, Coach Grayson, you can give up now." Cash glanced around at the chaos, shoulders lifting. "Or I can't do anything to help you."

"You boys really are oversized teenagers, aren't you?"

Eyes narrowing under the brim of his white University of Texas baseball hat, Cash lunged for the sprayer at the same time she squeezed. Water bounced off his rust-orange Longhorns T-shirt, spraying everywhere. He switched tactics, wrapping boa constrictor arms around her from behind. Her grip on the sprayer weakened. Though she prided herself on being in shape, she was no match for him.

"Ready to give up yet?" The proximity of Cash's voice sent tingles down her neck.

Olivia risked a glance over her shoulder. Laugh lines rimmed Cash's eyes, and unlike Sunday, all of his attention was on her. She was enjoying it way too much. Though the phrase *Rachel's brother* sounded like a referee's whistle in her mind, Olivia just shook her head in answer to Cash's question, letting her legs go out from under her. The self-defense move allowed her to drop down and out of Cash's hold.

Janie yelled for Olivia to get out of the way, then threw a bucket of water at Cash. Olivia popped up laughing. Janie only came up to Cash's chest, so most of the water landed on his previously dry cargo shorts.

"Jack, get your woman," Cash yelled to his friend as he resumed the tug-of-war over the hose with Olivia.

Feeling the sprayer slip once more, Olivia shouted for Janie to run as Cash gained control of the hose. Instead of escaping, her friend lurched onto Cash's back, not accomplishing much in the way of help but totally getting points for effort.

Cash let loose, spraying Olivia point-blank. Water ran from her face and neck, soaking her red tank top and athletic shorts. She sputtered, coherent enough to see Jack peel Janie off Cash's back and throw her over his shoulder.

Not above using a ploy when the need called for it, Olivia sank to the ground and cradled her foot. She didn't whine—no need to overdo it. The water stopped and Cash dropped to one knee beside her.

"Are you okay?"

Ugh. Did he have to look so irresistible? Water dripped across his cheeks, wet eyelashes accentuating one of his best features. His neck and shoulders tensed, ready for the water that might come at them from any direction.

It sounded as though a war raged around them, but Olivia didn't see anything but him.

His hand paused inches from her face, as if he intended to wipe the water from her cheeks. Her breath stalled in her chest, then came out in a whoosh of disappointment when his hand lowered.

"Did you hurt your foot?" Cash slid callused hands along her bare skin, her flip-flops doing little to interrupt the current that flowed between them.

His touch was too much. Olivia lunged forward, tackling Cash while screaming for her team at the same time. Though he could easily throw her over his shoulder like Jack had done to Janie, she managed to catch him off balance. Cash fell back onto the asphalt, taking her down with him.

With a war cry, her team descended, Rachel in the lead. Though they aimed for Cash, they managed to get Olivia just as bad. By the time the onslaught ceased, Olivia found herself cradled on Cash's left side, water running into her ears, hair plastered to her head and neck, clothes soaked through again.

Cash's hand tightened around her arm, holding her captive as his head dropped to the ground. "Shh." He whispered against her hair. "If we're quiet, they won't know we're down here. Play dead."

Shaking with laughter, Olivia left her head in the crook between Cash's arm and chest.

"Well, Coach Grayson." His casual drawl made her grin. "I think that one backfired on you."

She peeked up from his chest, and he returned her smile with one of his own. Olivia hadn't had that much fun in…she didn't know how long.

"I wouldn't say it was a total loss." Olivia laughed as Cash ran a hand through his hair and water flew out in every direction. Sometime during the scuffle, he had lost his baseball hat.

Janie and Jack approached as she and Cash moved to a sitting position. The Smiths sat beside them, and the four of them caught their breath while the students finally called a truce.

Jack shook the water from his hair like an overgrown puppy. "What are you guys up to tonight? Do you want to come over for dinner?"

Hadn't she just talked to herself about this very scenario?

Cash stiffened beside her and found his soaked cap on the ground behind them. He snapped it on his head, then stood. "Thanks, but I can't. I've got to run."

The three of them stood, too, the confusion Olivia felt mirrored on Jack's and Janie's faces.

"But you didn't get your truck washed." Olivia squeezed a hand down her ponytail, releasing a barrage of water.

He dug out his wallet and pressed a somehow still-dry twenty into her damp hand. "For the team." Then he jogged to his truck and pulled out of line.

Olivia stared after him, not quite sure what to do with the feelings coursing through her. The hurt from Colorado flashed back, memories of Josh walking away almost suffocating her. She could still see the positive pregnancy test and the two that followed with the same little plus signs. And then…the stress, the shame, the miscarriage.

Olivia had strayed from God's waiting-for-marriage plan. She'd walked away from God. And her decisions had ended in heartache and regret.

Watching Cash drive away—experiencing that tinge of hurt at his quick disappearance—for the first time in her life, Olivia actually felt momentarily thankful for her jaded past and all those regrets. They kept her from letting her heart get involved with a man who didn't even know it existed.

Just like the last time.

Chapter Four

❧

Cash stirred the chili bubbling in the pot, then checked his watch again. The first day of after-school practice had been over for hours and still no sign of Rachel. And of course she hadn't responded to his call or texts. He sighed, laid the wooden spoon on the holder and headed for the cordless phone. He dialed Trish Nettles's number, hoping the girls had lost track of time and were holed up in Valerie's room doing homework.

Yeah, right.

"Hello?" Trish sounded hurried. And why wouldn't she? It *was* dinnertime. For normal families.

"Hey, Trish, any chance Rachel's at your house?"

"I haven't seen her since practice." And now she sounded sympathetic. "I'll walk down to Val's room to see if she knows anything."

A seed of worry planted itself in Cash's gut.

Trish's voice mixed with Val's as a stench filled the kitchen. Cash hurried back to the stove and clicked off the burner for the now-scorched chili, turning on the fan over the stove to help remove the awful smell.

"Val doesn't know where she is." Trish paused and he slid open the window behind the sink. "Last I saw Rachel, she was talking to Blake Renner after practice."

The seed in Cash's stomach twisted into a full-grown ash tree.

Before they hung up, Trish made him promise to call if he needed any more help finding Rachel. The Nettles family joked that Rachel was their second daughter because of all the time she and Val spent joined at the hip. Maybe they should keep her full-time. Trish would be a much better parent than Cash.

He set the chili pot into the sink, flipped on the water and gripped the edge of the counter.

Renner. What did Rachel see in the cocky boy? He only wished her whereabouts were more of a surprise.

Cash scrounged up some leftovers and tried to distract himself with the Monday-night Rangers game, but nothing held his attention. Each tick of the clock increased his anxiety, and the food sat like a rock in his stomach.

He and Rachel had one steadfast rule between

them—always let me know where you are and where you're going. The stipulation wasn't that hard to follow. He'd had a similar rule with their parents, but he'd never pushed the way Rachel did. Mom and Dad hadn't known how good they'd had it.

When the Rangers game finished, Cash checked the time again. Almost ten o'clock. His phone showed three reception bars, but still nothing from Rach. He texted her again. He'd give her another ten minutes before he got in the truck and started looking. Cash's fingers slid down his contact list, landing on Coach Grayson's number.

The out-of-town area code flashed on the screen and then disappeared as he contemplated making the call. She was Rachel's coach. Maybe she knew something he didn't.

Though Olivia probably wasn't very happy with the way he'd acted at the car wash on Saturday. He'd had to run, had to get away from how simple it would be to let her in. Jack and Janie loved her. Being with her was too easy. So he'd scrambled out of there, needing some distance.

She'd been in church again yesterday—without Gil—but Cash hadn't talked to her. Somehow, he needed to figure out a way to be friends with her and nothing more. When his parents passed away, he'd promised himself that he'd give Rachel his undivided attention until she graduated from high school and went to college. No dating. No distractions. He owed Rachel the same great upbringing he'd had, the same love and support he'd received from their parents. After all, if Cash hadn't believed Tera the day of his parents' deaths, Rachel's life would have had a different outcome.

The familiar mixture of responsibility and determination weighed down his shoulders, and Cash let out a slow breath. He'd managed not to date for the past four years. Surely he could handle one more.

Cash pressed the send button for Olivia's number. He wasn't going to throw away all of those years of effort in one phone call.

"Hello?" A door closed in the background as she answered. Had he interrupted her evening? What was he thinking? Of course he had.

"Hey, this is Cash. I—"

"Oh, hi." Her voice held curiosity, and surprisingly after how he'd acted on Saturday, a hint of warmth that stopped his train of thought for a few seconds. "Is there anything I can help you with?" She filled in the silence, but she didn't have to fill in the rest of the sentence. Cash could hear the words as if she'd said them: *at ten o'clock at night… on my cell phone.*

"Rachel hasn't come home yet tonight. Any chance you might know where she is?" A commercial flashed on the TV at a high volume and Cash grabbed the remote to mute it.

"Sorry." Sympathy laced the word. "I haven't seen her since the end of practice."

Disappointment clogged his throat. "Sorry to bother you on your cell."

"It's not a problem."

"How was the first day of school?"

At Olivia's silence, Cash checked the cell to make sure they hadn't gotten disconnected. He pressed the phone back to his ear. "I'm giving Rachel a few more minutes to show up. Distract me. Tell me about your day."

"Oh." Olivia paused and Cash envisioned her shrug. "It was the typical craziness of the first day. The kids were hyper and excited, and I got very little done besides handing out a list of assignments for the quarter. I did tell my advanced class that we'd be speaking only French in the classroom this year."

"How'd that go?"

"They all complained." A smile echoed in her words. "So, tell me about your day."

He ignored the way his heart hitched. "I did a bunch of work in the office. I needed to get the website updated with what cuts we currently have available."

"No roping and riding today?"

He laughed. "Nope. Just office work. Have you ever even been to a ranch?"

"I've driven past one. There's a bunch of them in Colorado."

Cash waited.

"But no, I can't say I've ever visited one on a field trip or anything."

Sassy thing. "I'll give you a tour when you come on Thursday night, city girl." Cash checked the clock. "I better go. Rachel still hasn't shown up. I'm going to call Jack and Janie and see if they've seen her."

"Wait. I was just over there for dinner and they were both home." Her voice lowered. "So…I don't think they've seen Rachel either."

He hated the relief that flooded through him when he realized she'd been at the Smiths'. Instead of what? Out on a date with Gil? Did it matter? He certainly couldn't ask her out himself. Obviously his attention needed to remain on his sister.

Cash grabbed his red Circle M baseball cap perched on the back of the couch and tugged it on his head. "Guess I'll hop in the truck and start looking." After clicking off the TV, he went in search of his keys.

"I'll help."

He stopped midstride, suspended in a strange time warp as Olivia's words hugged him. "You don't need to do that. I don't want to keep you out late and—" *Rachel's my responsibility.*

"I won't take no for an answer. She's my player." Her words halted for a moment. "And your sister."

Maybe it wasn't all about Rachel. Maybe it had something to do with him. Cash moved again, collecting his keys from the kitchen counter and a flashlight he hoped he wouldn't need from the drawer.

Since his parents' deaths, he'd only focused on Rachel and the ranch. It felt like basking in warm sunlight to think Olivia might possibly be interested in *him*.

Cash tamped down his rampant thoughts. One offer to help and he went crazy with ideas he should not be entertaining.

Time to head back to Friend Land, Maddox.

On that note, he should say no to Olivia's help, but he couldn't resist the idea of someone keeping him from thinking worst-case-scenario thoughts while he looked for Rachel.

"I'll swing by and pick you up."

"Um, how do you know where I live?"

Cash laughed. "I'm not a stalker. You're three houses down from Jack and Janie in Mrs. Faust's above-garage apartment. If you wanted anonymity, this isn't the town for it."

At Olivia's silence, Cash checked the connection again. He put the phone back to his ear in time to hear her quiet, forced-sounding laugh.

"Right. Wasn't thinking about the size of this town. I'll head down when I see your lights."

Cash stepped onto the porch, locking the door behind him. "Make sure it's me. I don't need to go searching for two girls tonight."

She laughed for real this time, the sound bringing a smile to his lips despite his rising level of stress.

"Are there even criminals in this town?"

"Yes, city girl."

Another laugh set his heart racing, but he ignored it as her words brought comfort of a different level. She was right about there being very little crime in Fredericksburg.

Cash strode across the yard to the garage, pausing when he saw round Wrangler-style headlights about a half mile down the road.

"Cash?"

"Hold on. I see some lights coming."

"Oh, good."

The Wrangler downshifted as it eased into the yard, and Cash's shoulders dropped a mile at the flash of sunshine-blond hair behind the steering wheel.

"It's her. Thanks for keeping me sane."

"No problem."

Cash couldn't resist checking. "I'll see you Thursday?"

"I'll see you Thursday." Olivia hung up and Cash disconnected.

If only his gut didn't roll with anticipation. Because despite the interest Olivia Grayson stirred in him, Cash wouldn't let his feelings progress beyond friendship.

He might be a poor substitute parent, but he would do everything he could to make up for that...including giving up any thoughts of a relationship with Olivia.

Tonight only proved his promise to keep his attention on Rachel and not on his own love life was right on the mark.

Maybe in a year he could ask Olivia out.

Right. As if she'd still be single by then. Someone as attractive as Olivia moving into this little town was front-page news. He wasn't the first man to notice her and, unfortunately, he wouldn't be the last.

On Thursday, Olivia turned when she saw the sign for the Circle M, taking a long dirt drive that led to a toffee-painted house with white trim. Off to the left, a line of trees bordered the house and to the right, a barn and garage were painted to match.

After parking to the side next to Rachel's Jeep, Olivia walked up the stairs, flip-flops echoing across the wide, wooden-planked porch that ran the length of the front of the house. Since the Texas heat and humidity didn't have an off button, she'd pretty much adopted a different version of the same outfit every day—shorts, T-shirt or tank, flip-flops or tennis shoes.

Guardrail spindles cast shadows onto two rocking chairs that moved in the breeze as she knocked.

"Hey, come on in." Cash greeted her at the door dressed in jeans and a black T-shirt, hair wet. He smelled like some kind of men's soap. Who knew such a simple thing could be so attractive?

Hands off, Liv. After their phone conversation the other night, Olivia felt as if she and Cash had moved into new territory—one where their focus centered on Rachel. Exactly where Olivia needed it to be. And she didn't plan to mess up this new-found harmony with any remnants of buried attraction to Cash.

"I'm warming up one of Laura Lee's lasagnas." Cash motioned to the table where Rachel had her homework spread out. "Have a seat and I'll grab you a glass of lemonade."

An expansive living room with high ceilings connected with the kitchen and dining space that held a round oak table. Summer evening sun came in through large front windows, playing upon the dark burgundy sofas that flanked a stone fireplace stretching all the way up to the second-story ceiling.

Olivia sat at the table next to the girl she'd seen at practice a half hour before. The one who had dominated in their first match last night with five kills and helped them win in only four games.

Rachel tossed her hair. "I can't believe Cash conned you into helping me."

Girl, I've dealt with plenty of teenagers like you in the past. You won't get rid of me that easy.

"It's all selfish." Olivia pretended nonchalance—though she couldn't stop a smile. "I just want you to keep playing volleyball."

A hint of a curve touched Rachel's lips, but she quickly quelled the movement. After rearranging her pencils and notebooks, she huffed and rolled her eyes. "I need help with algebra the most."

Perfect. Olivia's worst subject. "Then let's get started."

While Rachel pulled out her book, Olivia glanced up and shared a small victory grin with Cash.

An hour flew by as Rachel and Olivia switched from algebra to English and then got in a bit of world history before Cash put a stack of plates on the table next to Rachel's papers.

"Ready in a few." He added silverware and napkins.

"I'm almost done." Rachel quickly scribbled in two more answers to her history homework before stacking up her books and papers and dumping the pile onto the floor near her chair.

When Cash put the lasagna on the table and took

a seat, laying his palm up next to Olivia's plate, she stared at the callused hand. Rachel accepted the other hand Cash offered her without an eye roll—shocking—and Olivia made herself do the same, trying not to think about how small her hand felt wrapped up in Cash's during the prayer.

They dug into the delicious meal, and after finishing off two full plates of food, Rachel disappeared from the table, cell phone in hand.

Cash leaned back and stretched his arms over his head, plate cleaned a few times over. "So, are you ready for that tour?"

"Sure." Olivia loaded the dishwasher while Cash put away the leftovers.

Cash slid on his boots, and they walked out the front door and over to the barn, the first signs of dusk seeping into the evening.

"Did you always plan to ranch?"

"Pretty much. Dad would have been fine with me doing something else, and I went to college open-minded, but I missed it. I moved back right after to work with him. Of course, I didn't know at the time that I'd end up doing it all myself. Except for Frank. Every day I thank God for Frank."

"How can you talk about your parents so openly? Doesn't it…"

"Hurt?" Cash filled in the word as his gaze swung in her direction. "Yep. But it gets a bit easier with time." He slid open the massive barn door and flipped on the lights. The fluorescents flickered before kicking on with a buzz. An organized wall of tools lined one side of the barn and the other housed a long row of horse stalls. By the names etched into wooden signs on the gated doors, it looked as though only a few of those were occupied.

A whine sounded from another area of the barn and Olivia paused, waiting to see Cash's reaction. Maybe it was nothing…or normal. She didn't have a clue.

His eyebrows pulled together, and he walked in that direction. Olivia followed, thinking everything Cash did had a calculated calm to it. The way his legs covered the distance communicated his concern, but he didn't rush, even waiting for her to catch up. Once she did, he turned and stepped through a small doorway and flipped on the lights. A desk pushed against one wall and rows of cabinets filled the squared space that Olivia could walk off in a few long strides.

"This is Frank's space."

When the whimper sounded again, Cash strode to the desk and dropped to his knees. "Hey, girl." His quiet soothing continued as he reached into the foot space of the desk and gently maneuvered a beautiful black-and-brown dog out into the light.

The dog's breathing seemed labored, and scratches marred her nose and face, including one eye that looked almost swollen shut.

"What's wrong?"

"I'm not sure." Cash ran his hands over the animal. "What happened, Cocoa?"

She answered with a high-pitched whine.

Olivia sank to the cement floor next to Cash, stomach churning when he swiped over the dog's shoulder and his hands came away covered in bright red blood.

"She must have gotten into a tussle with something. She'll be all right. I just need to clean her up and then wrap up that spot on her shoulder."

"You're going to do it yourself?"

When Cash grabbed a rag from one of the cupboards above them and wiped his bloodstained hands on it, Olivia pressed her lips together and looked away.

"Yep." He looked at her, amused. "But that doesn't mean you have to stay."

Cocoa whimpered and scooted over, depositing her head in Olivia's lap. Any reservations Olivia had about staying were forgotten. She took over for Cash's soothing, running her fingers over the soft fur behind Cocoa's ears and along her back—anyplace she didn't seem injured. "If you're staying, I'm staying."

Cash disappeared into the other part of the barn, coming back with a handful of supplies. He cleaned the wound on the dog's shoulder first.

"See? It's not very big. I think I can wrap it up tight instead of doing stitches."

Olivia slammed her eyelids shut when Cash attempted to show her what he was doing.

He chuckled. "Not much for blood?"

"You could say that." Again. Olivia continued to soothe Cocoa as Cash applied topical anesthetic and then ointment to each of the scratches across the dog's face. Cocoa didn't flinch or move at Cash's gentle and efficient movements. But when he moved to the open wound, she whimpered and looked up at Olivia with one good eye, pain evident.

"It's okay, sweet girl. In no time at all you'll be running around again. He's almost done." Olivia glanced at Cash. "Aren't you?"

Cash continued his ministrations. "Yep, but if you keep up all that sweet talk, Cocoa's going to milk this thing some more and find a few more injuries to complain about."

Olivia ignored the warmth cascading through her at Cash's words and his close proximity, instead focusing on the beautiful animal in her lap.

After wrapping a bandage around Cocoa's shoulder, Cash secured it with medical tape. "There. All done. Now we just have to make sure she keeps the thing on." Cash rubbed Cocoa behind the ears. "Do you hear me, girl? No chewing."

The world tilted. Olivia threw a hand out to the cool cement floor, hoping to steady herself. Surely she wouldn't faint now.

Cocoa moved her head to the floor as if she could sense Olivia's unease.

"Olivia?" Cash knelt in front of her, studying her much like he had Cocoa only minutes before. "Are you okay?"

"I'm fine." She forced a smile to her voice and her face. "You have two heads, but other than that, I'm good."

She needed to get out of this barn and find some fresh air. Olivia popped up and the walls swirled and spun. She imagined shoving her feet down through the cement floor in order to steady her swaying body, but instead, two warm arms wrapped around her. She let her face rest against Cash's soft T-shirt and rock-hard shoulder as the scent of that soap surrounded her.

How many times could she end up in this man's arms by accident?

She was afraid the answer to that question was not nearly enough.

Cash should let go. Olivia seemed better, but his own pulse raced as though he'd just run across miles of ranch land. What was it about this woman that messed with him? He'd been attracted before, but not like this. It unnerved him the way she seemed all soft and sweet one second and then toed up to his sister in attitude the next.

Wanting to comfort, Cash allowed himself to slide a hand down her satin hair one time, releasing the scent of her mint shampoo.

"Doing better?" He ducked to look into her face.

She nodded, not meeting his gaze, then stepped away. He clenched his fists to keep from reaching for her again.

"I need to go." Olivia walked outside and Cash followed, turning off the lights and sliding the barn doors shut behind them.

Under the newly darkened sky sprinkled with stars, Olivia paused and took a few deep breaths. The vastness of the charcoal backdrop and the quiet night left Cash feeling as though they were the only two people in the world.

Not exactly what he needed right now.

"Thanks for dinner." Olivia's quiet voice interrupted his off-limits thoughts.

"Thanks for helping my sister."

"You're welcome."

Cash decided she looked a little less green. "Do I need to drive you home? Or follow you?"

She laughed. "I can drive myself home and no, you don't need to follow."

"Are you sure? Because I don't want—"

"I'm fine." Olivia ran a hand through her hair, sending the tips dancing across her light blue V-neck T-shirt. "It usually only takes me a few minutes to recover. I can drive. I promise."

They walked to the house and Olivia retrieved her purse. Cash stood on the front porch and watched as she drove away, thinking the new volleyball coach had revealed something to him tonight that he'd never realized in all the years he'd lived on the ranch.

He could be jealous of his dog.

Chapter Five

Olivia knocked on the Maddoxes' screen door the next Thursday, the sounds and smells of dinner wafting into the evening. An afternoon thunderstorm had provided a break from the stifling heat, and she welcomed the slightly cooler air whispering across her skin. Olivia had seen Cash a few times this week—at a fund-raising event, church and last night's game. Amazingly, she'd managed to avoid falling into the man's arms for the past seven days. The two of them had also kept any conversations at parent-teacher level and mostly centered on Rachel. Now, if Olivia could just keep up the same track record tonight.

"Come in," Cash called from the kitchen and Olivia let herself in, finding him taking a pan out of the oven. And no sign of Rachel. Hopefully the girl was just upstairs…though now that Olivia thought about it, she hadn't seen her Jeep outside.

Cash set the pan on the stove and threw her an apologetic look. "It seems my sister has decided she doesn't need any help tonight. She never showed up after practice. I'm sorry. I would have called you, but I hoped she was just late."

Olivia took a step backward. If Rachel wasn't here, then she had no reason to stay. "No problem, I'll just head—"

"To the table." Cash strode across the kitchen, placed his hands on her shoulders and propelled her into a chair. "You drove out here. The least I can do is feed you."

When Cash went back to the stove, Olivia resisted popping up from her chair. She shouldn't stay. Not if Rachel didn't need her help. But…what if the girl showed up and Olivia had already left? She should probably give her a few minutes.

Cash tossed a blue-and-white crocheted hot pad on the table and then moved back toward the counter. "Tell me about your day."

Olivia shoved down the swell of sweetness that phrase caused her to feel.

"After last night's win, I thought practice would go great. Instead, the girls were distracted messes. I'm not sure why. I made them run lines for the last fifteen minutes. Guess I should call my dad and get some advice."

"Is he a coach?"

"Yes. At a college in Colorado Springs."

Cash whistled. "Now it all makes sense. Were you born with a volleyball in your hand?"

"Not quite. I didn't start until fifth grade. At that point, I was already inches taller than the boys in my class. I decided to take advantage of it."

He set the steaming glass pan on the table along with a container of sour cream and bowl of guacamole. "You're in for a treat. Laura Lee makes the best enchiladas."

"If the smell is any indication, I believe you." Yum. Cooking for herself, Olivia hardly ever took the time to make anything that looked or smelled like this.

"But I'll have you know, I prepared the guacamole myself."

Olivia grinned and nodded toward an empty plastic container on the counter. "Really? Looks like Wholly Guacamole made the guac to me."

Cash filled two glasses with water and ice from the fridge door. "I didn't say I *made* it. Just *prepared* it." He approached the table, expression suddenly serious. "Lying is not something you'll ever catch me doing. I am not a fan." His voice took on an edge that Olivia had never heard before.

Interesting. Olivia wasn't a fan of lying either, but she didn't feel the need to say it out loud.

Cash placed the water glasses in front of their plates, his mischievous smile returning. "I took the guacamole out of the freezer, where Laura Lee put it, defrosted it and put it into a bowl."

Olivia laughed. "Since that's more than one step, I'll give you two points."

"Accepted." Cash sat to her left and reached for Olivia's hand. She startled, having forgotten this habit of his, then tried to catch up when he bowed his head to pray. He acted as if this hand-holding thing were no big deal, as if it shouldn't make her heart crawl into her throat and miss the prayer completely. When he finished, Olivia picked up her fork and said a silent prayer of her own before digging into the food.

Their conversation during dinner didn't require any effort. It just felt…easy. And wasn't that the problem with this man? But she was here to help Rachel, not fall further into friendship with Cash. Although Rachel taking herself out of the equation made that hard to accomplish.

After eating, they cleared the table together and Olivia prepared to leave. Since Rachel hadn't shown up, Olivia didn't have any reason to stay.

She grabbed her purse while Cash put the leftovers in the fridge. He turned. "You ready? Wait, where are you going?"

"Home."

Cash walked over and tugged the purse from her arm, setting it on the table. "I still owe you a tour, city girl. Remember? We didn't get to finish it last time. Instead, we got to witness all of the reasons you never became a nurse."

She laughed and narrowed her eyes. "We can't all be Janie."

He grabbed his boots from next to the front door, pulling them on while Olivia wavered with indecision. She really should go home to her empty apartment.

"Jeep or horse?"

"What?"

"A real tour requires some sort of transportation. And since my lovely sister has decided not to grace us with her presence, we have plenty of daylight left. So which chariot do you prefer? Jeep or horse?"

"I'd say horse, but I wore flip-flops." Huh. Guess she'd made that decision rather quickly. So much for sticking to all-Rachel business.

Cash studied her feet, making her skin flush with heat. Who knew feet could blush?

"I'll be right back." He disappeared into the back of the house and reappeared with a pair of camel-colored cowboy boots that had to be Rachel's.

Olivia sat on a chair and tried them on. Amazingly, they fit. Bless Rachel for having big-girl feet.

"Are you sure Rachel won't care if I wear these?" She stood and chuckled at her outfit, consisting of a light yellow tank top, cutoff jean shorts and boots. Thankfully she hadn't worn capris today.

That would be an unusual combination. "This looks hilarious."

"She hasn't worn them in ages. And they actually look...good on you." Cash glanced to the side as red climbed his stubbled cheeks. "Before you know it, I'll be changing your nickname." He moved to open the screen door, holding it for her.

They stepped onto the front porch, the gorgeous evening greeting them. Olivia inhaled the fresh, after-rain scent.

"Have you ever been horseback riding before?"

"A couple of times."

"I mean other than one of those ride-in-line-behind-each-other, follow-the-leader sort of things."

The corners of her mouth lifted. "That's the kind I've been on."

"And there went your chance for a new nickname." Cash gave a dramatic sigh as they walked to the barn. "Such a city girl. At least tell me you know how to bait a fishing hook."

There was a way to do it? "Nope."

"Horseback riding, fishing." He tsked. "What else am I going to have to teach you?"

"I'm guessing not anything about being humble."

He threw his head back and laughed.

They entered the barn and Cash saddled two horses. He ran a hand down the nose of the gray one. "This is Rachel's horse, Freckles. She's sweet."

Freckles nuzzled Cash's neck at the compliment. "And should be easy for you to ride."

Cash helped Olivia up and then mounted his own rust-colored horse. They rode at a slow pace toward the hills. Cash brought her up to a fenced area where it looked like hundreds of longhorns grazed.

"This is our herd. We're all grass fed from start to finish, which means we rotate the grazing often so that they get new grass. No corn, no grain. We don't use antibiotics or hormones. The care of the animals is more expensive, but then our meat also brings in a higher price. And it's healthier."

"Where do you sell it?"

"On the website and locally. We supply a few restaurants in town. Some families have been buying from us for thirty years. Right now I'm working on a deal with a natural grocery store down in Austin. If it comes through, we'd need to increase our herd."

Cash started off again, and the two horses walked alongside each other.

"So, what did you do back in Colorado? Besides win volleyball games like a boss and teach French?"

Olivia smiled. "I hung out with friends and my sister, Lucy. She still lived in Colorado Springs for college the last few years while I lived in Denver, but we saw each other a lot. And I used to mentor a group of high school girls. Some of my team went to my church, so they were in my Bible study." And what a stellar leader she'd turned out to be. Tension coiled down her spine. Last school year she'd quit being a mentor and kept to herself. Leaders were supposed to be an example of what to do instead of what not to do.

"You mentored teenage girls." Cash said it more as a statement than question, and Olivia managed a nod, though she didn't know what the fuss was about.

"You have to help me with Rachel."

She'd already agreed to tutor Rachel. What more did the man need?

"I don't have a clue how to help her, how to deal with a teenage girl, and you have all of this experience. You'd be perfect."

Perfect was not the word that came to Olivia's mind.

"It would be so great if you could give me advice. I'm desperate to figure out how to help Rachel out of this rebellious stage she's in."

"You don't ask for much, do you?"

Cash flashed a charming smile in answer, and Olivia's resolve weakened.

"I'm not sure what kind of help I would be. It's not like I have a counseling degree or anything."

"It doesn't matter. You are a chick."

"Thank you for that observation."

At her dry tone, Cash laughed. "Trust me, I've noticed." He cleared his throat, looking at the trail in front of them before glancing back to her. "And you obviously have a desire to help teenage girls. I get the feeling you can't resist the thought of saving one from trouble."

Now that part was true.

"I think it's the least you can do with me letting you tutor Rachel for free."

Olivia laughed. She needed to say no. She didn't need to add another thing that forced her into spending time with Cash. Plus, the thought of helping Cash with Rachel only reminded Olivia of her own mistakes. She wanted to start fresh, not act like a CD stuck on repeat.

"If tonight's any indication, I obviously need help with her." Cash punctuated the quiet statement with a shake of his head, then grew silent, leaving Olivia to her own thoughts.

Could God be showing her, once again, that her purpose in moving to Texas wasn't just to run from the memories? Despite how unqualified she felt, she could offer Cash some insight into the mind of a teenage girl. Olivia might not be able to erase her story, but the possibility that she could help write a young girl's into a better path of some sort…how could she say no?

Freckles dropped back as the path narrowed, following behind Cash's horse as they wound past a patch of scrub oak and started a slight climb.

"Hey." Olivia called ahead to him. "This looks and feels a lot like those other horseback riding tours I've been on."

His low chuckle floated back to her. "We'll save the racing and jumping fences for another day."

After about fifteen minutes, they reached a clearing. Cash dismounted and helped Olivia down. They walked to the edge of the hill. The path they'd taken wound through the trees below, the setting sun casting yellow, orange and pink streaks across the sky. Although there were no mountains to greet her, the green land and trees had a peaceful beauty all their own.

"It's so quiet. It's like another world."

"Yep." Cash stood beside her, looking out at the land with pride.

"Would you ever want to go anywhere else? Move anywhere else but here?"

"No. If you had all of this, would you?" His gaze never strayed from the view.

Her eyes stayed on the man next to her. "No." She sighed. "I wouldn't." Olivia pretended to check her watch, though the exhausted yawn that followed wasn't fake. "I'm sorry to cut this short, but I should really get going."

Cash helped her back onto Freckles, and on the ride back, every step of the horse under her seemed to aggravate Olivia's frustration. She should have stuck to her original plan. She should have gone straight home when Rachel didn't show up instead of talking to Cash as though they were friends. Because all tonight had accomplished was a growing ache in her chest. Their conversation about her life in Colorado had acted like a shovel, digging up a grave of memories that weren't buried deeply enough. If Olivia hadn't miscarried, she'd have a three-month-old right now. And while being a single mother wouldn't have been ideal, she *would* have made it work. Her love for that child had been instant. When she lost the baby, her feelings had bounced from mind-numbing grief to relief that the baby wouldn't be born into the mess she'd made. And that relief came with its own sense of guilt. How could she be okay with losing a child at all? But *okay* definitely wasn't the word she would use to describe how she'd felt about it then or now.

Before she'd met Josh, she used to dream about a man exactly like Cash for a husband—kind, Christian, hardworking, good sense of humor. She stole a glance at him riding next to her, drinking in the way he looked at home in a saddle. His strong jawline jutted out, a touch of concentration lining his forehead as he watched the fences along their path. Definitely not a chore to look at the man.

But the combination of it all only amounted to one thing: regret. Though she'd hoped her move would leave behind the guilt and shame she'd experienced in Colorado, it had hitched a ride shot-gun and taken up permanent residence in her new life. And until Olivia figured out how to move beyond those chains—until she could forgive herself for the past—she had no business dreaming about the future.

Rachel came down the stairs as Cash finished his second cup of coffee. She was dressed for school, hair and makeup done. If only she didn't wear such dark stuff around her eyes. But he had to pick his battles. And the one about to go down weighed in as more important.

To say he'd been furious last night when Rachel didn't show up would be an understatement. Cash had spent an extra hour rubbing down the horses after Olivia left, using the time to calm down and pray for wisdom and patience. After, he'd come inside to find Rachel in her room, listening to her iPod as though nothing had happened.

Jaw clenched tight, he'd walked away without saying anything, knowing he couldn't handle a conversation right then.

Thanks to a good night's rest, he felt as if they might be able to talk in a civilized manner this morning. Maybe Rachel had a good excuse. After all, she was a young girl grieving the deaths of her parents, not just his little sister driving him nuts.

Rachel's toast popped, and she spread peanut butter on it before dropping into the chair across from him.

Cash twisted his coffee cup back and forth, slowly releasing the air from his lungs. "We need to talk about last night."

"I know." Rachel's blond eyebrows scrunched together, her tone petulant.

Guess the night of sleep hadn't improved her mood.

Cash kept an even tone. "Where were you?"

"I forgot it was Thursday and that I was supposed to be here for tutoring."

Did he believe that? He didn't know. He only knew he was tired of fighting with the girl across from him. He missed his little sister. The one who looked up to him instead of glaring at him.

"Were you with Blake?"

Rachel took her sweet time before nodding. At least she still told him the truth about that.

"Rach, do you think I want to get on you about this stuff? Coach Grayson takes time out of her schedule to come help you. She doesn't gain anything out of it, and she doesn't get paid for it. It's offensive for you not to show up."

Rachel's perma-scowl softened and her chin lowered. "I know. I'm sorry."

Before Cash could even begin to hope, those green eyes flashed with defiance and she crossed her arms. "Coach Grayson only comes because she wants to see you. I did the two of you a favor by leaving you alone."

Cash barely kept from groaning. "That's not true and you know it." His little sister also knew just how to push his buttons. Resisting the temptation to argue further with her, Cash popped up from his chair and strode to the sink. His coffee cup clattered against the stainless steel while his body hummed with tension, craving the release physical labor offered. He stomped across the kitchen and out the door, boots kicking up dust as he crossed to the large garage next to the barn. If he was going to get so much guff over Olivia, he should at least be able to date the woman. But no, he got the worst of both worlds. No Olivia and a snarky sister to boot.

Watching the sunset last night, Cash had fought the temptation to let his mind wander into more-than-friends territory. Thankfully Olivia had cut the evening short. He might have promised himself not to date anyone while raising Rachel, but in truth, no one had tempted him until now.

Even Jack had noticed, ribbing him when they'd gone fishing on Saturday.

"So, are you going to ask the girl out or what? I'm beginning to think you're a perpetual bachelor."

The jab felt a little too close to the truth.

"Is this about Rachel?" Jack had been the only

one who'd put up with Cash after his parents' deaths, the only one to continually pull him out of the black abyss he'd fallen into. His friend deserved an answer, though Cash didn't feel much like giving one.

"Isn't it always?"

"It doesn't have to be."

"Yes." Cash had released a deep breath as the truth of what he'd said ricocheted through him, confirming once again what he already knew. "It does."

What Jack didn't understand—what no one fully understood—was that Cash owed Rachel.

If he'd stuck to his original plans the day of his parents' accident, his mom would still be alive, possibly even his dad. Rachel would have the best mother in the world to guide her and Cash wouldn't be left struggling to give Rachel the life she deserved. The life he'd had.

So, yes, it *was* about Rachel. And it needed to be.

Which meant Cash had to ignore how amazing Olivia had looked throwing a pair of boots on those toned legs of hers. He shook his head, wishing Olivia's appeal would fly out of his mind with the motion.

Unfortunately, that didn't seem like a viable option. So Cash had come up with a different idea. In order to help him keep his promise, he needed to tell Olivia about it. Maybe if he was honest and up-front about everything, it would make sticking to his plan easier.

All of this for a teenage girl who cared about nothing but herself. One he loved more than his own life. Cash's parents had given him a great childhood, lots of attention and a house filled with love and laughter. Why couldn't he give Rachel the same? Days like this made him miss his parents so much that he physically ached.

He climbed into the dusty ranch Jeep and started it, then stared at the wheel, a plan beginning to form. Turning off the ignition, he jumped out and switched to his truck, pulling up to the front of the house just as Rachel came down the porch steps.

He motioned for her to open the passenger door. Surprisingly it stayed connected to the vehicle when she did. "What?" Anger drew a line through the light smattering of freckles on her forehead.

"Get in."

"What for?"

"I'm driving you to school."

Her mouth swung open far enough for Cash to see the empty spots where her wisdom teeth had come out last year.

"You're kidding."

"I wish I was. I don't have time to cart your butt around, but I don't have any other choice. Somehow, you have to figure out that your actions affect other people. You can have your Jeep back on Monday."

"No." Rachel whispered the word as her eyes squeezed shut.

Cash tried not to enjoy the look of panic and despair that filled her face. "You better get in or you're going to be late."

Chapter Six

Olivia finished correcting the last period's papers and stacked them in her box for Monday.

"Coach Grayson?" Rachel Maddox slunk into the French room.

"Hey, Rachel. What's up?"

Valerie Nettles stood in the hallway, and Olivia waved at the less dramatic girl while she waited for the one standing in front of her to speak.

"I—" Rachel stared at her shuffling flip-flops. "I just wanted to say sorry for not showing up last night. I forgot, but I know that's not an excuse."

Olivia barely resisted a smile at the forced apology. "It's okay. Are you going to be there next week? Because I really don't want to hang out with your brother any more than necessary."

Olivia had hoped for a smile from the teenager, maybe even a laugh. Instead, Rachel crossed her arms. "Yeah, I will." Her sulky demeanor softened a touch. "Thanks."

The quiet word surprised Olivia. "No problem. I'll see you at the game tonight?"

"We'll be there. See you later, Coach." Rachel caught up with Valerie and the two of them disappeared down the hall.

Olivia stood and stretched, glancing out her window toward the parking lot. A group of kids stood in a circle with two squad cars parked near them. Unease slithered down the back of her neck. She hurried down the hall and pushed out the door, using a hand to shade against the bright sun.

The students seemed calm. Most of them milled about talking to each other. Cheerleaders had signs ready for when the football team came out of the school to load the bus.

Olivia approached one of the squad cars and waited as the officer rolled down his window. It couldn't be too bad if he was still in his car.

"I'm one of the teachers here. Is something wrong?"

The gray-haired man pointed a thumb over his shoulder. "Just waiting for the bus. We escort the football team and the student cars that follow."

He *must* be joking. Olivia managed to say thank-you and back away before giving in to her laughter. A police escort to a football game? Only in Texas. These players were treated like rock stars. She turned to go back inside, running smack into someone.

"Sorry." She took a step back. "Didn't mean to bowl you over. I—" Olivia's words stopped. The supermodel from church adjusted the belt over her frilly bright green shirt that cascaded down to long toothpick legs in skinny jeans and wedge sandals. She tossed fiery red hair and flashed bright white teeth.

"It's okay, sweetie, don't worry about a thing." Her voice had a syrupy quality that made Olivia resist a cringe. "I'm Tera Lawton, and I've been meaning to introduce myself to you. Seeing as how the whole town knows you've arrived and who you are. I'm the dance team coach. It's a part-time thing in the afternoons and evenings, so I'm not around during the school day."

Pity. Olivia chided herself for the bad attitude. "It's nice to meet you." She took a step to the right, wanting to get back to her classroom and away from the sugary-fake personality in front of her.

"Wait." Tera touched Olivia's arm. "I've seen you talking to Cash and thought you might want to know…" She leaned closer, as if the two of them were friends sharing secrets. "He's quite the heart-breaker. With you being new in town, I just thought I'd give you a warning so that you don't get hurt." Tera's lower lip slipped into a pout. "I mean, we wouldn't want our new French teacher to leave town with a broken heart, would we?"

Olivia didn't have words. At least, not ones she would voice. Janie had told her Cash had dated this woman. If so, Olivia didn't need to fear that he'd ever be interested in her. She and Tera were nothing alike in personality or looks.

The woman's eyes narrowed before she smoothed her features and flashed another fake smile. "Anyway, if anyone knows about the man, it's me. I thought you'd want to know his nature before you got more—" she tilted her head "—involved."

Olivia wanted to scream that she and Cash weren't dating, that they were only trying to help a struggling teenager, but Tera wiggled her fingers and took off across the parking lot, corralling the dance team into cars.

She walked back to her classroom, Tera's words sending a shiver of recognition down her spine. The girl was right. Probably not about the heart-breaker part, as Olivia couldn't see Cash being that way, but the bitter beauty queen had brought a truth into the light. Under the guise of helping Rachel, Olivia's heart could too easily slip and slide toward Cash.

And that wasn't something she could let happen. Not with her past hanging over her like a thunder-cloud. Olivia wanted to find the forgiveness and healing she knew God had already granted but that she couldn't seem to grasp.

She needed to feel new. So far, she was still waiting.

Which meant she needed to keep a tight leash on her growing attraction to Cash. Since she'd already started tutoring Rachel, she would follow through on that. But Cash's request to help him with his sister?

If it meant spending even more time with the man, Olivia just couldn't do it. She had to back away.

The Fredericksburg High School Billie Goats went for a two-point conversion and Cash cheered when they scored. For most of the first half, his gaze had bounced from his little sister—wearing a number eighty-two jersey and cheering for Blake—to the football game to Olivia and Janie sitting in the front row with Tucker.

Cash had allowed Rachel to ride to the game and back with the Nettles family since she didn't have a vehicle at her disposal and he wasn't mean enough to make her ride with him. She would have melted the seats in the truck with all of that anger. Trish had promised to get Rachel straight home after the game. Who knew, maybe some of Val's even-keeled nature would rub off on Rach tonight. Like it hadn't done for the past seventeen years.

At halftime, Cash headed from the visitors' section to the concessions stand. He talked to a few people on the way, and by the time he reached the line it almost hit the bleachers.

He resisted a groan when he recognized Tera's trademark red spirals in front of him in line.

Maybe if he took a step back and—

"Cash." Tera spotted him and practically purred. "You're just the person I wanted to see."

Shocking.

"I've been having all this trouble at my house." She threaded fingers through her hair in a move that looked practiced as a haze of overpowering perfume surrounded them. "My kitchen sink keeps leaking. I've been under it a bunch of times, but I can't get it working right. I wondered if you might be able to swing by some time and take a look."

Did Tera really think a line like that would work? Did she think anyone believed her lies? Hard to comprehend that the girl's honey-smothered southern drawl had once been attractive to him. Now it made his skin crawl. Cash extracted his arm from Tera's clawlike grip with a shake of his head. How did she get her nails into him so quickly? "Not going to happen, Lawton."

Tera's eyes narrowed, and Cash turned and scanned the crowd. One day she'd finally get that he wasn't interested. Would never be interested.

The fact that she thought something could be possible between them still amazed him.

Olivia approached the line behind him, and Cash couldn't help his grin or the relief he felt in seeing an honest, friendly face. She looked cute in khaki shorts and a red Battlin' Billies T-shirt, ponytail swinging across her shoulders.

When she spotted him, Olivia froze a few steps away.

"Hey." Cash tugged on the brim of his cap.

"Hey, Cash. How are you?"

Not that great if he counted Olivia's formal tone or the way she looked everywhere but at him.

"I better go find Janie."

"Didn't you just get in line?"

She shifted from one foot to the other. "Yeah, but I think Janie needs me."

What was going on? Why was Olivia acting so strange?

Cash pointed past her shoulder. "Actually, Janie's right behind you."

"Hey, y'all." Janie hiked Tucker further up on her hip and approached the two of them. "Tuck's been fussing the whole game, and I think maybe he's getting his two-year molars. The boy's a hot mess." Janie flashed Olivia an apologetic look. "Liv, I'm so sorry, but I think I better take him home."

Olivia rubbed a hand across Tucker's back. "It's not a problem. I don't mind leaving."

Cash glanced between the two girls, his gaze landing on Olivia. "I can drive you home if you want to stay."

She waved away his offer. "I'm fine going—"

"Cash." Janie perked up, interrupting Olivia. "That would be so great. I absolutely do not want Olivia to have to leave the game. If you guys see Jack, let him know we left. I'll send him a text for later but I don't want him wondering. Thanks!" Janie waved and took off for the parking lot almost at a run, Tucker bouncing on her hip, diaper bag swinging from her shoulder. The woman sure seemed in an all-fired hurry to leave, but then, if Tucker didn't feel well, Cash could understand that.

The concession line moved forward and Tera peeked around Cash.

"Looks like we're finally moving." Fake surprise dashed across Tera's face. "Olivia, it's so great to see you again."

When did the two of them meet?

Olivia greeted Tera and then didn't follow the line as it inched forward. "You know, I don't think I want anything anymore. I'll meet you at the bleachers."

"I'm good. I'll go with you."

By the time they made their way back to the visitors' section, the second half had started. Olivia sat as stiff as if she'd ridden bareback yesterday. She cheered; she talked to other people.

She just didn't talk to Cash.

When Tera climbed the bleachers, she glared at Olivia the whole way up.

Cash sighed. Now everything made more sense.

Olivia concentrated on the headlights cutting through the pitch-black night instead of the man across the truck cab from her.

Janie. Olivia couldn't believe her friend had bolted like that, leaving her with Cash. Now what was she supposed to do? She'd have to tell him that she couldn't help with Rachel any more than tutoring. But how would she explain that?

You see, Cash, I'm attracted to you and I don't want to be. I need time to work through my past, and I can't help your sister because I don't want to be around you more than necessary. Sound good?

She resisted a snort.

Instead of taking her home, Cash drove to the Dairy Queen drive-through. Olivia opened her mouth to protest, then changed her mind. While the need to escape remained, the desire to drown herself in a Blizzard won out.

"What would you like?"

"Heath Blizzard with chocolate ice cream."

Cash didn't raise an eyebrow. He ordered hers and a meal for himself plus a shake.

"I didn't have time to eat dinner before the game," he explained.

Then why had he gotten out of the concessions line with her? He must be starving.

They got the food from the window and Cash backed into a parking spot. He grabbed the bag. "Come on."

Cash hopped out of the truck and went around to the back, where he unlatched the tailgate and took a seat. Olivia had no choice but to follow. She pushed open her door, moving at a much slower pace. At the rear of the truck, she pulled herself up on the opposite side of the tailgate.

He offered her a fry, which she declined. Death by chocolate sounded much better.

Cash scooted back and twisted sideways across the truck bed, stretching his legs out. Wearing jeans, gray tennis shoes and a vintage Billies T-shirt that had to be from his own high school football days, the man still managed to look drop-dead you-know-what.

Annoying habit of his.

"Is that a grass-fed burger?"

Cash laughed, choking on his bite. "No, city girl. It's not." He took a sip of his shake. "Every so often I partake of a corn-and-grain–raised burger like the rest of the world."

Olivia's lips quirked up without her permission.

"I see you met Tera. I assume an apology is in order."

The grin fell off her face. How had Cash figured that out?

"If I know Tera, the meeting wasn't pleasant."

"Do you know Tera?" Olivia ate a bite of ice cream and cringed at the jealousy in her voice. Did she need any more proof that she should be backing away from Cash?

"Unfortunately, yes." His sigh echoed between them. "We dated during high school and into college. When I moved away for school, Tera stayed here. I found out when I came back on break that she'd been cheating on me. When I confronted her about it, at first she denied it. But eventually she admitted it and we parted ways."

Olivia had been right. She and Tera were nothing alike. Sympathy prompted her to peel her clammy thighs from the tailgate, scoot back against the opposite side of the truck bed and stretch her legs parallel to Cash's. "I'm sorry."

"Trust me, it was for the best." He crumpled the hamburger paper and tossed it in the bag. "That wasn't the only thing Tera and I disagreed on. She never shared my desire to…wait."

Wait? As in wait for marriage? Olivia's heart broke a little bit hearing those words.

"My parents always talked about it, and I know that's part of why they had such a great marriage." He shrugged. "I just want to do things God's way."

"Me, too," Olivia whispered. She hadn't done

things God's way in the past, but she wanted to now. If only she had never walked away from her beliefs, from God. If only she'd run from Josh instead of letting him in. But she knew better than anyone that *if only*s could crush a spirit.

"If it was just the cheating and breakup between Tera and me, I'd be able to let things go. But it didn't end there. After college, I moved back to the ranch. Tera would try to gain my attention in town, but I didn't have any interest in her anymore. One day she called saying she was sick and needed someone to get her a few things from the store. I wondered why she'd called me, but then, she didn't have that many friends left in town. I was supposed to go to Austin for a cattle auction with my dad, but I decided to check on Tera instead. Unfortunately, I was far too loyal back then."

A thread of tension seeped into the conversation, and Olivia set her ice cream down on the metal truck bed.

"When I got over there, I found out she wasn't sick at all. She just wanted to convince me we should get back together." Cash's fingers dug into the back of his neck. "I was upset with her for lying. We fought and I left." His gaze lifted to meet hers, and the pain there stole Olivia's breath. "Because I went to check on Tera, my mom decided to go with my dad to the auction that day. On the drive back that night they were killed."

"I'm so sorry." Olivia didn't have words for that kind of regret.

Cash took a minute before continuing. "Now you know why I can't stand lying. It's the one thing I can't forgive. It hurts too many people, and it never ends well. Rachel knows it, and so far, I think she's always told me the truth." He shifted one ankle over the other, taking a drink of his shake.

"After losing them, I had so many questions. What if I'd gone? Would I have been driving? Would I have seen the truck and avoided the accident? At least if I'd gone, my mom would still be here to raise Rachel. But now Rachel's stuck with me. I need to give her a good life, the life she would have had if my parents were still alive." Cash's shoulders lifted. "It's sort of like a volleyball game. I don't want to take my eye off the ball—Rachel—for one second. I don't want to have any regrets or wonder if I could have done more. I promised after our parents died that I wouldn't date until Rachel was out of high school and on her way to college. I promised myself that Rachel would get my undivided attention."

Gracious. Olivia swiped under her eyes. She could understand that. She could get behind that kind of commitment.

"That's why I keep asking you for more. I hoped you might be able to help me understand Rachel. Or give me advice. I'm not even sure what I'm asking for in terms of her. I guess I just need…something. Some help. And she does, too."

Olivia had thought she needed to back away from Cash in order to stop her feelings from growing, but now that she knew he didn't plan to date, it made everything so much easier. She could help him with Rachel and take the time to sort through her past without the possibility of a relationship developing between them. Knowing he had a promise to keep made Olivia relax for the first time since she'd met Cash. As long as they'd both made the decision not to date, they could actually be friends. And with how much they saw each other, that sounded far better than her previous plan.

"I'm not sure how much help I'll be, or what advice I have to give, but I'll do everything I can to help her. And you. I'm officially on Team Rachel."

Her conscience threw up a red flare at the way Cash's answering smile made her stomach do a cartwheel, but she ignored the warning sign and the sensation. With both of them on the same page, she felt confident she would stick to her plan.

Unlike the last time.

Chapter Seven

Olivia woke to a sense of foreboding.

Strange. Shouldn't she feel good about how the evening had ended with Cash? Their conversation last night might have come after a bit of turmoil and tension, but in the end, Olivia felt so much better about helping Rachel. She even felt peace about being friends with Cash.

They had come to an understanding, and Cash had given her another great reason to keep her heart from falling for him.

After their first conversation, she and Cash had spent an hour talking about how to help Rachel. The man definitely had his heart in the right place. Somehow he'd figure out what to do with the girl, if not by experience then by sheer determination.

Olivia had come home, put on *You've Got Mail*, which ran on a loop in her DVD player, and fallen asleep on the couch. Sometime during the night she'd shuffled from the sofa to her bed.

Now, she shrugged off her white down comforter along with the niggling apprehension and padded through the small living room that connected to her even smaller kitchen. The apartment had the basic appliances, including a dishwasher and a window air-conditioning unit that did a surprisingly good job of keeping her place cool.

Olivia fumbled with the coffee filter and grounds, gasping when it hit her.

The enormity of what she'd done made her stumble to the whitewashed table under the kitchen window and sink into a chair.

She'd said she agreed with Cash's decision about waiting for marriage…which she did.

But it sounded as though she'd made the same one…which she hadn't.

So now, added to her long list of sins, was a lie she hadn't even known she'd told. And now that she knew how Cash felt about lying, telling the truth would be all the more painful.

Tucker threw a tractor across the sandbox and then giggled. Olivia tried not to laugh with him, but the boy was incredibly cute.

"Let's not throw, Tucker."

He threw another toy and chortled again.

"Do you want to swing?"

The adorable monster picked up a cup and didn't respond. Olivia grabbed his hand before he could toss it and helped him dig into the sand. It distracted him and he began to dig and dump, dig and dump. Olivia brushed her hands against her denim capris to remove the sand, then twisted her hair to one shoulder of her black tank top, wishing for a breeze to cool them off.

This morning, Janie had shown up at Olivia's door to go dress shopping for tonight. Jack had managed to keep the anniversary plan a surprise, and Janie had been smiling even wider than usual.

"Girl, I can't believe you didn't tell me. You're supposed to have my back."

"Like you had mine last night at the football game? How's Tucker's tooth, by the way?"

Janie had grinned, shoulders lifting in innocence. "Better overnight."

The woman needed to give up on her matchmaking ideas, especially since Cash and Olivia were both in agreement on not dating.

As for Olivia's lie of omission last night with Cash…even after processing all day, she didn't know what to do about that. Truthfully, she wasn't ready to talk to anyone about what had happened between her and Josh. The man had walked away from her when she told him she was pregnant, saying he didn't want a family—even though they had talked about a future together. And then while she'd been dealing with the miscarriage on her own, he'd started dating another teacher at the same school. All last year she'd had to work with both of them while her heart continued to bleed. That kind of hurt didn't mend easily, nor did the constant ache of wondering if her stress had caused her miscarriage.

But despite the fact that she didn't plan to discuss any of that with anyone anytime soon, the question remained…would Cash consider what she'd said last night—or hadn't said—a lie?

Tucker scooped another cupful of sand, and she ran a hand along his soft hair. Though being with him reminded her of the baby she'd lost, Olivia knew his sweet personality also brought healing, and she was all for that.

Tucker lifted the cupful of sand and tipped it to his mouth. He got half into his mouth and down his throat before Olivia smacked it away. Wheezing, Tucker tried to breathe through the particles blocking his airway.

Olivia grabbed him and flipped him so that he faced down. She dug into his mouth, pulling out sand as fast as she could. When she got most of it out, he continued to choke and wheeze. She flew into the house and ran the water in the kitchen sink. Would wetting the sand make it better or worse? She didn't have a clue. Tipping him forward again, she began the same process, this time with water.

Finally, he sputtered and caught his breath.

Olivia set him on the counter next to the sink and helped him drink a few sips of water. It must have loosened the last of the sand from his airway, because he started splashing his bare feet in the sink.

Olivia's knees swayed. What if she hadn't been able to help him? What if Tucker—?

Bracing her hands against the counter on either side of Tucker as he played, Olivia took a few deep breaths and tried to calm her nerves. When her heart stopped pounding in her ears, she cleaned the sand off Tucker's hands and feet, dried them with a paper towel and then picked him up.

"Time for dinner." With shaky arms, Olivia put Tucker in the high chair and gave him a bowl of applesauce and a plastic spoon. He went to work on that while she warmed up his peas and noodles.

When she turned back, Tucker had applesauce in his eyebrows and spread across the tray. She switched the bowl out with the plate in her hand, and Tucker immediately sent peas flying across the kitchen.

So she could pretty much count herself as the worst babysitter *ever*.

The doorbell rang and Olivia checked to make sure Tucker was buckled into the high chair before going to answer.

Through the glass storm door, she could see Cash standing on the front step.

She swung the door open, answering his confused look. "Jack and Janie are gone for their anniversary dinner. I'm babysitting." A crash sounded in the kitchen. "Come on in."

Olivia arrived in time to see Tucker dump the last of his noodles over the side of the tray, like the dump truck he'd just been playing with in the sandbox.

Cash followed her into the kitchen and raised one eyebrow. "Who won the fight?"

"Tucker." Olivia surveyed the small turn-of-the-century kitchen with bright red cabinets that had been clean minutes before. "Definitely Tucker."

"Need some help?"

More than you know. "I need to give him a bath and clean up this mess."

"Which one do you want me to do?"

If Cash gave Tucker a bath, Olivia couldn't harm the poor kid any further.

"I'll take kitchen duty. Although, he's hardly eaten."

"No problem." Cash fed Tucker a big bowl of applesauce, a banana and a plate of noodles in a matter of minutes. Show-off. Then he pulled Tucker from the high chair and flew him into the bathroom while Olivia switched from sweeping up peas to wiping cupboards.

From the sound of the commotion and fun happening in the bathroom, the bathwater would be all over and not just in the tub. She smiled at the banter between Tucker and "Unc Cas." Cash sure knew his way around a kid. Maybe because he was so much older than Rachel. Olivia *would not* dwell on what an attractive quality that was in a man.

What was Cash doing here, anyway? Olivia hadn't even asked. She'd just put him straight to work.

She finished cleaning the kitchen and headed down the hall in time to catch Tucker's flight from bathtub to changing table.

Cash laid him down, and Olivia put on his lotion and diapered him. They managed to get the squirmy monkey into pajamas and into his crib. He sucked his thumb, staring up at them with curious eyes.

Olivia and Cash shared a grin before turning on Tucker's mobile and sending stars dancing across his darkened ceiling. They moved down the hall and into the living room.

Cash leaned against the back of the chocolate couch Janie referred to as pleather and braced his hands beside him, stretching his heather-brown T-shirt across muscular shoulders. Tonight, he wore jeans and boots—a slightly different casual look than last night. Same effect.

"Thanks for the help."

"You're welcome. I don't know how Jack and Janie keep up with that boy."

"Me either. He almost needed an ER visit tonight, and I was sitting right next to him." As

Olivia told Cash the story, the reality of what could have happened made her body feel as limp as one of Tucker's cooked noodles.

Cash barely bent to look into her eyes. She loved that he had to do that. "You do know he would have done the same thing with Janie or Jack here. It wasn't your fault."

If only that statement could apply to the rest of her life. "I'm not sure about that, but I am glad he's okay."

"Me, too." Cash glanced at the front door. "I guess I better get going. Janie texted me this afternoon and asked if I could come by and look at her car tonight. Weird, huh? Especially with them being gone for their anniversary. Did they drive her car or Jack's?"

"Hers." Olivia bit her lip. She was going to have a talk with Janie about her matchmaking. Two nights in a row was a step too far, though the thought did make Olivia hold back a laugh. How could such a sweet bundle of energy like Janie have such a plotting nature? "She didn't mention anything to me."

Cash shrugged. "Maybe she meant to say tomorrow night."

Not even a chance. "You fix cars too?"

"I can usually pinpoint what's wrong, at least. Mechanical work is not Jack's strong suit."

Despite Janie's interference, Olivia was actually thankful for Cash's presence. He'd helped her with Tucker and made the end of the evening go much better than the first half. "Since you're here, do you want to hang out? I'm just waiting for Jack and Janie to get back at this point. They'll be gone late. We could watch a movie or something."

Cash paused before answering, and Olivia felt sure he'd head right back out the door. Just as she started to regret asking, he nodded. "Sure."

Her shoulders relaxed. "I'll make popcorn. You choose a movie."

Torture. Cash knew of no other word that could more perfectly describe watching a movie with Olivia. After putting Tucker down, she'd pulled her hair up into a ponytail, and her tanned shoulders and black tank top did little to help him concentrate on the TV.

He didn't even know what movie he'd picked. Some chick flick. Cash had guessed Olivia would like it, but her laughter told him it had comedy as well. He had watched a little, more enjoying the sound of her amusement than the movie itself.

His and Olivia's conversation last night about Rachel and not wanting to date had ended well. Until he'd gone home and realized that saying and doing were two different things. Olivia's personality, combined with an athletic body and striking blue eyes, wasn't easy to ignore.

But that's what Cash needed to do. He didn't have any choice but to keep her firmly in the friend category.

He'd thought telling Olivia about his promise would make things easier, but the conversation hadn't taken away that *something* in his gut that said he could be missing out on his future. Last night he'd even found out that Olivia believed the same things as him.

She had all of the qualities he wanted in a wife, and Cash couldn't pursue a relationship with her. He felt trapped in some kind of self-imposed prison. But he could be confident he was following God's will in regards to his promise about Rachel. At least he had that.

The movie ended, and Olivia leaned forward, digging in her purse by the foot of the couch. She took out a red egg-looking thing, twisted it open and slid it across her lips.

Something strawberry and sweet bombarded his senses. *Mercy.* The woman needed to stop smelling so good.

"What did you say?"

He *had not* said that out loud. "I said…that smells good. What is it?"

"Lip balm." She held it in front of him. "Want some?"

Yes. He did. But he wanted the application to come from her lips. It took everything in Cash not to lean forward and find out if her lips were as sweet as she smelled. How long had it been since he'd kissed someone? Years. But he knew absence had nothing to do with the desire to kiss this woman.

"I'm fine. Thanks." *Fine*. Right.

Cash needed to focus on something besides Olivia. He could always think about his sister—like he should be doing anyway. Yep. That worked for dissolving his way-past-friendship thoughts.

He shoved off the couch and stood. "I'd better go. I'll see you at church tomorrow?"

Olivia nodded just as the front door opened and Jack and Janie spilled over the threshold. Janie had a look of amusement—and was that victory?—on her face and Jack had one of shock.

"Date night?" Jack switched to a grin, and Cash barely resisted rolling his eyes like Rach. Sure, he and Olivia had watched a movie together, and yes, he'd thought once or twice about holding her hand. After seeing her yawn, he'd even wondered if Olivia might fall asleep against his shoulder—but none of that had happened.

Although the situation did look a bit like a date. Cash could only imagine the months of ribbing that would come from this moment.

Jack's amusement increased, but he turned to Olivia instead of Cash. "When you said you wanted to hang out with your favorite little man, I thought you were talking about Tucker."

Pink raced up Olivia's cheeks, and she looked as if she wanted to climb under the couch. Funny. It wasn't like her not to have a witty retort for Jack.

The overwhelming urge to protect Olivia from Jack's teasing prompted Cash to say his good-byes and move to the front door. Maybe tomorrow morning he'd head to church early. He'd sit in the sanctuary, listen to the music before the service and talk to God about this whole mess. Maybe God could help him remember that being friends with Olivia didn't give him a free pass to let his feelings grow. Because despite his and Olivia's conversation last night, Cash could use a reminder.

A scuffling noise sounded on the church roof, and Olivia glanced at Janie. Her friend shrugged in answer to Olivia's silent question, mouth twitching. Last night, after the embarrassing end to the evening with Cash, Olivia had talked to Janie about her matchmaking. She'd agreed to stop, but this morning the woman couldn't keep the amusement off her face. Had Olivia realized Jack would tease her just as much, she would have considered skipping church.

Good thing she hadn't. The sermon was on forgiveness today. Could there be a better day for her to pay attention? But as Pastor Rick read through the parable of the unmerciful servant, the scratching noise sounded from the roof again and again.

"Search your heart. Have you forgiven those who've sinned against you? Have you forgiven yourselves? Some of you find it easier to forgive others but forget that includes you."

Gracious. Olivia could answer both of those questions with one word: *no*.

How did God do that? How did he take a sermon meant for the whole church and make it speak directly to her? Olivia knew she needed to forgive Josh and herself. She just didn't know how to accomplish it.

At the end of the service, people filtered out, most still talking about the noises on the roof.

Olivia and Janie walked to the back of the church. Jack had gone out during the service to see if he could help figure out what was going on. Now he stood near a group of teenagers, along with Cash, a few other parents and a bunch of church staff members.

Janie pulled Jack aside. "What's going on?"

He glanced at the group before taking a few more steps away. "That noise during the service was a bunch of teenagers up on the roof."

Janie frowned. "How did they even get up there?"

"I don't know. I'm guessing there's a way up somewhere for maintenance, and they must have found it. Thankfully, no one got hurt."

"That's such a relief." Olivia scanned the group until she spotted Rachel. "Was Rachel one of the kids?"

"Yep."

Olivia's stomach rolled. Cash would be irate. He'd been mad about Rachel skipping out on tutoring—and that was small potatoes compared to this. When the circle of teenagers and staff started to break up, Olivia headed for Cash and pulled him to the side.

"Are you okay?"

"No." Worry lines covered his face. "What am I supposed to do with her?"

Olivia resisted reaching up to smooth away the stress marring his features. If only she could help.

"Can you send her home and give yourself some time to cool down?"

"What? I can't. I have to discipline her even though I'm running out of ideas in that department. She's already without a vehicle."

"You asked me for help with her, and here it is. Let her be for a bit. Take a break and calm down. She'll be even more worried about what you're going to do and you'll have some time to think. Let's do something…go for a hike, maybe. We'll see what we can come up with together."

Cash's gaze landed on Rachel and his lips pulled into a thin line.

"I can't." He stared past Olivia as though she

didn't even exist. "I just can't let it go like that." After shaking his head, Cash released a deep breath and went over to Rachel. Seconds later, the two of them left the church, leaving Olivia struggling for her own answers.

Wasn't she supposed to be helping him? Hadn't he asked her for advice?

Though she attempted to shake off the dismissal, it hurt far more than it should.

Janie came over carrying Tucker and he lunged into Olivia's arms. She hugged the small, squirmy bundle as though he could make all things new. But he couldn't do that for her. Only God could. And after all of this time and all of her prayers and efforts in that regard, she still didn't feel as if she was moving forward.

If anything, today felt like a big step back.

Had she forgiven Josh? No.

Had she forgiven herself? No.

Was she a help at all to the struggling teenage girl she'd pledged to support?

Another big fat no. Her team might be winning volleyball games, but Olivia felt nowhere near a victory.

Chapter Eight

"Hey, Cocoa." Olivia bent to greet her friend, who lay sprawled across the Maddoxes' front porch. She scratched behind Cocoa's ears, grinning at the leg that started tapping against the wooden planks. The cuts on Cocoa's face seemed to be healing. Olivia could hardly see them anymore. And the one on the dog's shoulder? She wouldn't be checking that one.

She knocked. "Come in." Rachel's shout came through the inch the inside door stood open.

Olivia walked in and set her things on the table. Instead of Rachel doing homework and Cash warming up dinner, the teenager stood by the stove.

"Dinner should be ready in a few."

"Do you need help with anything?"

"No, thanks. Cash is working or something, so it's just me and you. I'm making mac and cheese." Rachel motioned to the blue box on the counter. "Sorry it's not much."

"It's plenty for me. I love mac and cheese." Olivia leaned back against the counter, an opportunity for the evening blossoming in her mind. Without Cash here, maybe Olivia could get Rachel to open up about her life.

They never had time at volleyball for Olivia to crack through Rachel's barrier. Plus, they actually had to accomplish something at practice. Last night they'd lost their first match. The Billies had played hard, but the other team had played better. It was the kind of loss Olivia didn't get too upset about. Although she was glad they'd meet the same team again later in the season. It would be nice to redeem themselves with a win.

"So—" Olivia's question got cut off when a huge commotion sounded outside. Cocoa started barking like crazy, and the spoon Rachel had been stirring with clattered across the counter.

Rachel flew to the back of the house and disappeared. Olivia followed, going through the mudroom and out the back door.

Outside, Rachel stood a few yards from what Olivia assumed was a chicken coop, yelling at the crazed Cocoa. Her legs were in a wide stance, hair flowing down the back of her blue T-shirt like some Wild West woman. Cocoa rushed around the structure excitedly, rotating between growls and barks.

"Cocoa. No." Rachel commanded the dog with a

strong voice, but Cocoa didn't listen. "She's going to get hurt. I'm going in."

"What?" *Into what?* "Rachel, what is going on?"

"There's something in there. Probably whatever tore Cocoa up the last time."

Olivia had to yell above the roar of dog and chickens. "You can't go in there. I'll go." She pushed past Rachel and ran to the coop, imagining her face would look something like Cocoa's in a few seconds. She wrenched the door open, then slammed it shut, hoping the noise would scare away whatever lurked inside. After yanking it wide open again, Olivia only made it a few yards back before a raccoon came flying out. Instead of running, it paused in front of her.

If ever there was a moment to faint, this was it. Beady black eyes stared her down, and Olivia's legs almost gave out, depositing her at eye level with the animal. Why hadn't she grabbed a stick or something to protect herself?

Had the raccoon just hissed?

Instead of acting large or intimidating or any other thing she'd ever heard about dealing with a wild animal, Olivia turned tail and ran in the other direction. She grabbed Rachel along the way and didn't stop until she reached the back of the house. Only then did she pause to turn back. She saw the back end of the raccoon as it disappeared into the tall grass.

"Cocoa." They both yelled at the dog when she took off after the raccoon. Thankfully, Cocoa came back. How could she not remember what had happened the last time?

Rachel grabbed Cocoa's collar and made her way into the house, leaving Olivia to follow at a much slower and shakier pace. When she passed through the mudroom, Cocoa whined at being confined to the space. Olivia gave her a sympathetic pat on the head, then made her way into the kitchen.

Rachel stood near the stove again. "I think I might have overcooked the noodles."

You think? "They'll be fine." Olivia helped herself to a glass from the cupboard and filled it with water from the sink. She drank the whole thing, then moved to the table and collapsed into one of the chairs. Her legs felt as if she'd just finished a three-day volleyball tournament in college.

Rachel, on the other hand, seemed completely calm. She got out the milk and butter, mixed the noodles with the cheese packet, and set the pot in the middle of the table. Two bowls followed.

"Fork or spoon?"

"Fork."

"I knew there was something strange about you."

Olivia choked on a laugh. Had ornery Rachel Maddox made a joke? She suddenly felt thankful for their facing-down-the-wild-animal experience outside. Maybe it would swing their relationship in a new direction. One where Olivia could actually help the girl.

They dished the food, and Olivia took a bite, trying to hide her distaste as a congealed glob of soft noodles filled her mouth. She looked up to find Rachel staring at her bowl, eyebrows pulled together and lips pursed.

The girl stirred her noodles with a spoon, then dropped it into the bowl with a clang. "That's disgusting."

"They're just a little overdone. It's not like you were standing over the stove watching them."

Rachel huffed. It seemed to be one of her favorite noises. "At least Cocoa didn't get hurt." She tucked a strand of buttercream hair behind her ear, her voice a whisper.

Olivia agreed with her. The girl had a heart. She just didn't want anyone to know it. "So…I assume you're never allowed to leave the ranch again?"

Rachel rolled her eyes, but her lips curved a bit. "Only for school and volleyball through this weekend. I hadn't even finished the last grounding when he took away my Jeep. He just tacked on another week."

Olivia didn't blame him. She had racked her brain all week trying to think of ways to help Rachel, but she kept coming up short. Cash already did so many things right. He ate dinner with Rachel most nights, went to all of her games, supported her in every way he knew how. Rachel just seemed to be some unsolvable mystery.

She looked down at the table. "I thought he was going to take away the homecoming dance. And I mean, crawling up on the church roof was not my best move, I'll admit that. But next weekend?" She looked up with such hope in those green eyes that Olivia's breath stuttered. "I really want to go. We got a limo and everything."

"Are you going with Blake?" Olivia would have to be in another country not to notice Blake and Rachel together around school, after practice, after the football games.

"Yeah."

"So where's your dress? Do I get to see it, or is it a surprise?"

At the last staff meeting, Olivia had been day-dreaming and gotten roped into chaperoning the dance. But she didn't mind. Since she was one of the few single teachers without kids, she could hang out with a bunch of teenagers for one night. What was the difference? She did it all day.

Rachel fidgeted with her napkin, studying the daisy print much longer than she usually studied her schoolwork. "I don't have a dress yet." She shrugged as if it didn't matter, but of course it did. "Cash wouldn't let me drive, and now I'm not supposed to leave again. I don't know when I'll have time to look. Mrs. Nettles asked me if I wanted to go when she took Val, but—" Rachel got up and cleared their bowls of uneaten macaroni and cheese, depositing them in the sink. "But I don't always want to crash on them."

"Can I go with you?"

The bowls clinked and Rachel glanced up. "You'd want to?"

"Of course. Where could we go?"

"There's a mall down in Kerrville."

That was where Olivia had gone dress shopping with Janie. "Is that all the way to Mexico?"

No laugh. No smile. Man, the girl was tough to crack.

"It's about thirty minutes."

"Is that the best place to go?"

Rachel loaded the dishes in the dishwasher. "We could go to Austin, but that's over an hour away. My aunt and uncle live there. We could stay with them, but then you wouldn't want to go."

Wouldn't she? Why not? What did Olivia have holding her here that Rachel's sad look couldn't pull her away from?

Rachel opened the freezer and took out a carton of mint chocolate chip, then got out two white bowls and set the items on the table.

After retrieving the ice cream scoop, she heaped a generous amount into each bowl. "Dinner is served."

When a fork appeared next to her bowl, Olivia

laughed. She got up to get her own spoon, thinking she had more in common with this teenage girl than she'd realized. Including a heart that needed some healing. After that sermon on Sunday, Olivia had decided to start praying more consistently about how to grant forgiveness. To herself and others.

She took a bite, pointing to the bowl with her spoon. "This is my kind of meal." The mint ice cream had shaved pieces of chocolate—Olivia's favorite—and she ate another spoonful before jumping back into the dress conversation. "I really don't mind going to Austin to shop. I think it would be fun. But how are we going to go this weekend if you're grounded?"

Rachel shrugged, the hurt back on her face.

"Check with your brother and see if he'll let you go with me. If he says yes, how about Saturday?"

When Rachel's lips lifted, Olivia resisted the urge to break into song. A Rachel smile earned her at least five points. Maybe ten.

If Cash searched Google for the word *exhausted*, his own haggard picture would pop up.

Over a dozen longhorns had escaped through a broken fence, it had taken most of the day to fix the water system *and* he'd been out working until ten o'clock and had missed seeing Olivia.

That last one shouldn't matter so much, but it did.

He entered the house through the back mudroom and took off his boots, then proceeded into the kitchen. The first floor of the house was quiet and barely lit, making him wonder at the whereabouts of his sister. Hopefully she hadn't sneaked out. He didn't have the energy for trouble tonight.

After downing a glass of water, he opened the fridge, leaning against the door as he rummaged for leftovers. He came up with a questionable-looking slice of pizza and flipped on the kitchen light to better examine it. No mold greeted him, so he took a bite. It couldn't kill him.

"Cash." Rachel's voice startled him.

She was sitting on the couch, earbuds in her hand as if she'd just plucked them out.

"Hey." Cash walked over to the chocolate recliner chair that partially faced the couch and dropped in. He set the piece of pizza on his jeans— now it probably *could* kill him—and pulled the footrest close. After propping up his feet, he let out a breath.

"Long day?"

"Never ending." He slapped a hand against his chest in mock surprise and looked over his shoulder. "Did my little sister just ask about my day? I must have walked into the wrong house."

Rachel snorted—the snotty kind, not the humorous kind. There went that sweet sibling moment.

She tossed her iPod onto the couch cushion and shifted forward. "Cash, a raccoon got into the chicken coop. It almost attacked Coach Grayson."

Pizza lodged in his throat and Cash coughed a number of times before he could speak. "Please tell me you did not just say what I think you said."

"It didn't, really." Rachel rolled her eyes. "I mean, Coach Grayson kind of…faced it down. Have a sense of humor, brother."

He'd definitely stumbled into some strange parallel universe.

"We were trying to scare it out before it got to the chickens and before Cocoa got hurt. She was going wild." She paused, looking as if she blinked away tears. Cash leaned forward, worry knotting his gut. What else had happened?

"You're going to have to…check the coop. I couldn't bear to look—"

"I'll take care of it."

He'd forgotten what a soft, sensitive thing she could be. Not that he wanted to deal with anything like that either, but still. Lately Rachel had been all brick walls, guns blazing.

"Cash, is there any way I can go shopping this weekend? I need a dress for the homecoming dance and—"

Cash tuned her out, hurt rippling across his chest. Just once he thought Rachel might be thinking about someone besides herself. But she only wanted a way out of her grounding. For climbing on the church roof, of all things. Truth be told, when he'd driven home from church Sunday, he'd held back a laugh. How did the girl come up with these crazy shenanigans? If it hadn't been dangerous, he really would have laughed—behind closed doors. But the fact that she could have been hurt?

Cash felt his own walls go up. Rachel was his responsibility, and somehow he would keep her safe. Even if he had to lock her up at home to do it.

Rachel finished her spiel. "So, can I go?"

"No." He stood, went to lock the front door, then turned off the kitchen lights. "No, you can't go."

"But I don't have any time next week. I have practice every night or a game, and then the dance is Saturday."

With each word, her pitch increased with panic. "I'm going to bed, Rach."

He ignored her screech and went upstairs. After showering, he climbed into bed, only wanting one thing. He wanted to call Olivia, to hear about her day, to have her voice be the last thing he heard before he drifted off to sleep.

But that didn't sound like friendship to him. So he didn't let himself call. Seemed it was a denying kind of night around the Maddox house.

* * *

"I'm trying to understand why he'd say no." Olivia clapped with Janie when the football team ran out on the field. Tonight's home game had the stands packed, the crowd wild.

Janie shifted Tucker on her lap and dug through the diaper bag until she found a toy car. He clutched it in his chubby hand and then whirled it across Janie's black shirt and down her red capris. "That's strange. It doesn't sound like Cash to be so harsh."

"I know." Olivia released a breath, wishing her frustration would go with it. "I'm not even sure what he said. Rachel came into my classroom this morning looking like her shuttered self. She didn't say anything other than that he'd said no."

Olivia couldn't be more confused. The man had asked her for help with his little sister, and the two times she'd offered, he'd refused. Why had he asked her at all?

"Speaking of…" Janie tipped her head toward Cash as he entered their row. When he reached them, Janie stood up to give him a hug. Olivia only managed a curt wave.

Usually Cash sat in the alumni section, but tonight he moved down the row until he sat next to her. When he nudged her right shoulder with his left, Olivia ignored the move, keeping her eyes on the field. Cash leaned into her line of vision, forehead creased, Billies baseball cap hitched up.

"What's going on? Rachel said you came out to the ranch last night."

Was the man joking?

"Um, yes, I did. Rachel and I met up with a raccoon, and then we ate ice cream for dinner and did some homework." *And then I got her to open up and you ruined it.*

"I heard about the chicken coop. Sorry about that, city girl."

"I have seen a chicken coop before. I'm from Colorado, not Manhattan."

Cash frowned and leaned back as though Olivia's words had physical power. The referee blew the whistle for the game to start and Olivia turned her attention back to the field. When Cash tucked a strand of hair behind her right ear, his touch made her jump a full volleyball off the bleachers. Was he trying to read her face or make her crazy?

"What's wrong with you? Everywhere I go some girl is mad at me. Rachel wouldn't even talk to me this morning."

"Are you surprised? You told her no for shopping this weekend."

"How did you know about that?"

"It was my idea."

"What?"

He looked so confused, it only made her more frustrated.

"I told her I would take her shopping. She

doesn't have anyone else, buckaroo. Do you think she wants to tag along with her friends and their moms all the time? Or have to go shopping by herself for a homecoming dress? I got the girl to agree and smile. Genuinely smile. She seemed excited. We talked about going to the mall or even down to Austin to stay with your aunt and uncle for a night. And then you swooped in and killed the idea even though you asked me to help her!" Olivia borrowed a huff from Rachel.

A slow grin spread across Cash's face, reminding Olivia of hot fudge melting ice cream. She wanted to grab a dishcloth and wipe it away.

"You are amazing."

What?

Cash leaned closer. "I didn't know any of this. I was exhausted last night, and I didn't hear everything Rachel said. I thought she was just being Rach and trying to get out of a punishment."

Olivia started to relax, realizing her shoulders were almost touching her ears.

"And she is still trying to get out of a punishment, but if it's to hang out with you, that's different. You're better for her than a week of grounding."

Her cheeks heated enough to set the field grass on fire.

Cash's low voice continued near her ear. "So, yes, Olivia Grayson, you can take my sister shopping. You can pretty much do anything you want and I'd be fine with it."

The idea Olivia had right now did not fall into the friendship category, so she shifted away a few inches, unable to stop the smile that spread across her face and the warmth that went all the way down to her tennis shoes.

Janie leaned forward and faced them. "Hey, you two, I don't know if you noticed, but there's a football game going on." She grinned. "And we just scored a touchdown."

Chapter Nine

Olivia plucked her iPod from the cup holder in the center console and passed it to Rachel. "Pick something out."

It took Rachel about ten miles to sort through Olivia's playlist and find something they could agree on—The Band Perry. Good thing Olivia liked country music or the state of Texas might very well drive her mad.

The teenager kicked off her flip-flops, tucking long legs beneath cutoff jean shorts. Her eyes closed as she crossed her arms over the *can you dig it* phrase on her bright blue T-shirt. The *O* was a small volleyball. Olivia would contemplate stealing the shirt if there was even a chance it would fit.

The sun shone down, she had a steaming cup of coffee in her cup holder and a half-grumpy teenager beside her. What more could she want?

For Cash to have hitched a ride along. Oops.

Today had nothing to do with Cash. Even though his words from the game last night still reverberated in her head, Olivia wasn't going to dwell on them. Or him.

Today was all about befriending Rachel and getting the girl to open up.

This morning before they'd left, Olivia had second-guessed agreeing to stay with Cash and Rachel's aunt and uncle for a night. That would make it look…as if she and Cash were in a relationship. Of course they weren't, but everyone in the town of Fredericksburg probably already thought they were. And now who knew what Cash and Rachel's aunt and uncle would think?

Olivia shook off the thoughts. God could handle it. *Hello.* She hadn't even prayed about it. Taking the time while Rachel stared out her window and presumably woke up, Olivia talked to God about the day and the girl. After, she felt peace. And when Rachel turned to her with a smile, Olivia thought they just might get somewhere today.

About an hour later, they turned into the driveway of a yellow house. A petite woman with short white hair flew out the door, arms waving. Dressed in lime-green capris and a flowing white shirt, she pulled Rachel out of the car and hugged her for a long minute. Rachel made introductions, and the next thing Olivia knew, she was enfolded in the same hug by Rachel's aunt Libby.

The woman leaned back and studied Olivia with a smile creasing her eyes, the hazel color reminding Olivia of Cash's. Gorgeous looks must run in the family.

"Aren't you cute as a button? Tall, but that's perfect for my nephew."

Olivia ignored the comment and the way Rachel looked up from her phone and scowled.

"You look like Cash. You have the same eyes."

Libby winked. "His daddy and I didn't look a lot alike, but we did share at least one feature. Come on in, y'all. I've got some lunch set out and then a whole day of shopping planned."

Olivia and Rachel shared a grin and followed her inside, leaving their overnight bags by the door.

"Hey, Uncle Dean." Rachel shyly hugged her uncle, who also wrapped her in a long hug.

"We missed you this summer, kiddo."

Libby turned to Olivia. "Usually Rachel spends a month with us in the summer, but this year she didn't want to leave her friends." Libby pretended to wipe away tears. "I don't know why that girl doesn't love us anymore."

Rachel giggled.

"I guess we're getting too old, aren't we, Dean?"

"Hey, I'm a year younger than you. Don't be calling me old."

Libby's hands landed on her hips. "And he'll

never let me forget it. How old are you, Olivia? If you don't mind me asking."

"Twenty-six. Soon to be twenty-seven."

"That's nice." Libby didn't say anything more, but Olivia could see her doing the math.

Too bad she couldn't answer Libby's unspoken thought out loud. *Yes, Cash is twenty-seven—older than me, not younger. And no, I don't see any loving, teasing relationships like yours in my near future.*

Libby poured glasses of sweet tea. "Let's eat some lunch. Then we'll leave old Dean here to his afternoon nap and get some girl time in."

An hour later, the three of them loaded into the car. Libby had a map with the stores outlined and a description of each one. "Rachel, look this over and tell me where you want to start."

Olivia smiled back when Libby's eyes crinkled in the rearview mirror.

"Aunt Libby, these are boutique stores. They're way out of my—"

"I don't want to hear it. I'm buying the dress."

"But I have mon—"

"Do you really want to fight with me?" Libby leveled a steel gaze at Rachel. "I know I come off all Texan and sweet, but I grew up on that ranch, too, little girl. Let me spoil you a little. You know all of your cousins moved out of the house and are long gone. At least give me this."

"You can buy me a dress," Olivia piped up from the backseat, and both Rachel and Libby laughed, easing the tension.

"Are you going to prom, too, Olivia?"

"It's homecoming, Aunt Libby."

"Right, homecoming."

"I am a chaperone, but I'm joking about the dress. I'll wear something I have."

Libby glanced in the rearview mirror. "We'll see about that."

The first stop was a swanky bridal store with a curtained dressing room area and a chandelier lighting the space. Olivia felt thankful she'd at least stepped up her typical shorts/tank/flip-flops combination to a multicolored ruffled tank top, tailored jean shorts and strappy flats.

Rachel walked the rows, choosing what she wanted to try on, and Libby and Olivia carted stacks of dresses to the dressing room.

They settled in to wait while Rachel tried on dress after dress. Rachel's opinions came quickly.

"Too pink."

"Too short."

"Too long."

"Not enough cleavage."

That one earned a tongue clucking from Libby.

"Too much cleavage," Libby announced on the next one and sent Rachel back to change again.

Oh, my. Thank You, God, for sending Libby on

this outing with us. Olivia wasn't sure she would have had the guts to tell Rachel anything was too short or had too much cleavage—even though it would have been true.

They put a bright orange dress on hold, then worked their way through three more stores in the area. By the fourth, Olivia needed a big chocolate bar, a coffee and a nap.

Libby approached Olivia with her arms full of dresses and tilted her head toward the dressing rooms.

"All right, Frenchie, you're up."

Olivia laughed. "No way. I'm exhausted just watching Rachel try on dresses."

Rachel came out of the dressing room in a blue number. "I don't like this dress, but I had to tell you not to mess with Aunt Libby, Coach Grayson. She won't take no for an answer."

Rachel glowed like a flower that had been fertilized with Miracle-Gro, and Olivia didn't want to do anything to take the happy off her face.

"Fine." She grumbled and took the pile of dresses, making Rachel and Libby laugh.

The first dress barely covered her derriere. Why did they make dresses so short these days? Or maybe it was that her legs were twice as long as the rest of the population. Olivia showed the second one to Rachel and Libby—a gold number that went to the floor. She received two *no*s and headed back in. She didn't like the third, but she showed them the flowing mint-green dress anyway.

"I like that one better, but it's still not great." Rachel's teenage tact made Olivia laugh. But she agreed with the girl. Rachel was in a different dress than the last time Olivia had been out—a black one this time.

"That looks great on you." It covered all the right places and swept down to the floor. "It's pretty."

"But it's black." Rachel's nose wrinkled.

They both retreated to their dressing rooms. Olivia pulled the last dress off the hanger. Short and sequined, the deep blue dress gave her hope. Not prom looking. Not old-lady looking.

No way would it look right on her. She tried it on, analyzing in the mirror. It showed off her legs but still looked modest enough for a teenage dance. Though sleeveless and quite simple, it had enough sparkle to be interesting.

Probably way out of her price range. Olivia dug the tag out of her armpit and tried not to dance. *Clearance.* Teacher-speak for *yes, you may buy.*

She flew out of the dressing room to a round of applause from Rachel and Libby. After they oohed and aahed, Olivia changed back into her clothes and then paid for her dress—refusing Libby's generous offer to pay.

She set her package on the floor and sat next to

Libby on the viewing couch, tempted to rest her head against the woman's shoulder.

"This is it!" Rachel squealed. Olivia had never heard the girl put so much excitement into anything before—even their near miss with a raccoon. Rachel flew out of the dressing room and stood in front of the three-way mirror, her eyes alight, a smile blooming across her face.

Her happiness took Olivia's breath away, and that wasn't considering the way Rachel looked in the dress. She looked like a princess. It was long enough that Cash wouldn't demand she stay home, had enough coverage in the front that she looked modest and was the prettiest shade of soft silver.

Libby swiped real tears. "I feel like you're getting married and we found the perfect dress."

They all laughed.

"Wrap that baby up," Libby commanded the dress attendant. "I need a highly sugared coffee."

Rachel headed back into the changing room while Olivia imagined a salted caramel mocha drenched in whipped cream flowing into her exhausted system. "I think you and I are going to be besties."

Libby laughed. "That's good, since you're going to be my niece."

Olivia's head jerked back. "I'm not—you do know that Cash and I aren't—"

"I know my nephew has some crazy ideas about

life. He thinks if he controls everything, he can give Rachel the same childhood he had. He can't make that happen." Libby sniffed again, fingertips checking for runaway mascara. "I'm an emotional mess. Just wait until your sixties, girl. Anyway, Warren and Sharon are gone and nothing is going to bring them back. Rachel's life isn't going to be the same as Cash's."

Libby's love for Rachel was obvious, and Rachel seemed so happy spending time with her aunt. Even her reaction to Dean earlier had been sweet.

"Why didn't you and Dean…?"

"Why didn't we raise Rachel?"

Olivia nodded.

"We talked about it. We prayed about it. But in the end, we all came to the same conclusion—Rachel was supposed to stay on the ranch. Even she agreed. So while I know she and Cash sometimes have trouble…"

Olivia snorted and Libby grinned.

"I think they're right where God wants them to be. Both of them. I also think that once my nephew figures out he can't control everything, he'll be knocking down your door. So be ready." Libby's mouth curved, reminding Olivia of Janie and one of her all-knowing grins.

Olivia didn't know how to respond to that, so she looked back toward the dressing room to check on Rachel. But instead of changing, Rachel stood a mere foot behind them, phone clenched in her fist. A scowl lined her face, replacing the pretty glow from only minutes earlier.

Had she heard their conversation?

By the way she gave Libby and Olivia the triple threat—crossed arms, rolled eyes *and* a huff—Olivia imagined she had.

Her stomach dropped down to her shopping bag on the floor. She'd had one plan today—shower attention on Rachel and get her to open up. Yet somehow she'd managed to make the teenager feel less than, or as if Olivia was here because of Cash instead of Rachel.

When Rachel stomped up to the counter, Libby stood, giving Olivia's arm a reassuring squeeze. "It will be okay."

If only Olivia believed her.

Val's jump serve careened off the other team's defensive specialist and into the stands, sending the team into wild celebration along with the rest of the gym. Olivia and Trish celebrated the win together, then gave their players high fives and hugs before heading over to shake the other coaches' hands.

Cash waved from the other side of the gym, and Olivia waved back. He didn't come over to talk to her, and she felt relieved. Rachel still seemed upset with Olivia from this past weekend. She'd hardly spoken on the drive home Sunday, leaving Olivia feeling awful about the way things had turned out. She'd just wanted to help the girl. Why did it have to be so hard? Now she understood how Cash felt.

When the gym cleared, Olivia packed up her clipboard and grabbed the bin of volleyballs to return to the storage room.

"Hey, Olivia, wait up." Gil Schmidt's voice made her stop and turn as he jogged over to her. "Great game."

"Thanks." She knew a permanent smile accompanied the word. Winning definitely ranked as one of her favorite pastimes.

"I hear we're both working the homecoming dance this weekend. That's what happens to the single teachers—we get the weekend duty."

She laughed, her mind going back to the dress she'd found. Could she really wear it? What would the other teachers be wearing? Maybe she should just save it for another time.

When are you ever going to need a dress like that, Liv?

For a friend's rehearsal dinner or wedding. That familiar ache lodged in her chest. Surely someone else would be getting married soon and Olivia would be carted back to Colorado to pretend that it didn't bother her to watch everyone else fall in love and walk down the aisle.

"So, what do you think?"

"What? Sorry, Gil. My mind was wandering."

"I wondered if you wanted to grab something to eat. I'm starving and thought maybe you didn't have time to eat before the game."

Her stomach growled in response to his question.

"Don't worry, I don't mean as a date. Anyone in this town can see you and Cash—"

"We're not dating." Her words sliced the air like a knife, but Gil just raised his hands and laughed.

"So, are you hungry?"

She was. And it would be nice to hang out with someone besides Cash for a change. Gil was easy to be around in a way that Cash wasn't. She wouldn't have to keep her feelings in check with the man in front of her. He looked cute in jeans and a green polo, making Olivia regret her hasty first impression of him.

Too bad he still didn't compare to the cowboy who'd recently stood across the gym from her as if a chasm stretched between them.

"Sure. Dinner sounds great. Just let me pack up my things."

Chapter Ten

You can't go. Cash clamped his back teeth together to keep from saying the words. When had his little sister grown into this beauty in front of him?

She and Val had been upstairs for most of the afternoon, commandeering the bathroom with more makeup, hair products and strange curling and straightening contraptions than he'd ever seen. He'd actually felt thankful to have a million things to do out on the ranch.

But now the two of them came down the stairs, smiling and looking far too old for their age. Cash swallowed the unwanted emotions in his throat. Rachel would not be okay with a big show of sap.

"You better take the gun, Rach."

Rachel grinned at the implied compliment, looking happier than she had all week. She'd come back from her trip to Austin with a scowl etched in stone on her face. Cash had expected her to come home happy. Or not as ornery as usual. But Rachel never ceased to surprise him. She hadn't said much to him about the trip, but he'd managed to learn that she had found a dress and that Aunt Libby and Uncle Dean were well.

And that was it.

Maybe Olivia had done a better job of getting through to her. Rachel needed a mentor in her life, and if Olivia was willing to take on that role, nothing would make Cash happier.

Except for the fact that it only made him more attracted to the woman. Hopefully it didn't show. After the match on Wednesday, he'd forced himself to leave without talking to her. As though he had something to prove. He sort of did—to himself and the town. Surely he could stay away from her for a few nights.

On Thursday, Olivia had come for tutoring, but she'd left after helping Rachel. Cash had let that slide—just like every other night when he got in from working and his fingers itched to pick up the phone and call Olivia. Somehow he managed to resist.

He still had some self-control left in his life.

"We're headed over to Val's house. Her mom wants to take pictures and the limo is picking us up from there."

Pictures. He knew he'd forgotten something. "Have Trish send me some." Cash moved to hug

Rachel—careful not to muss her hair or dress—surprised when she accepted the gesture. "You look beautiful, sis. Just like Mom."

She blinked quickly. "Thanks."

Cash chuckled when Val and Rachel climbed into the Wrangler, hiking their dresses up to make it in and showing the flip-flops on their feet. He'd seen a few bags go into the Jeep and imagined their other shoes were in there. Not that he knew for sure.

Rachel jumped out of the car and flew back up the porch steps, looking like the little girl he remembered from before their parents' deaths.

"I forgot something." Up the stairs she went, leaving Cash stunned at the memories. Rachel's face had been alight, her smile wide. He'd like to see it that way every day.

Back down the stairs she came with a tiny purse in her hand. "I can't wait to see Coach Grayson in her new dress." Rachel came and went like a breeze, stopping in front of him to pop up and peck a kiss on his cheek. He felt as if a bull had knocked him over.

"Thanks for letting me go shopping last weekend."

"No problem."

"Did you know Coach Grayson is dating Mr. Schmidt?"

What? The strangely timed statement stole all of Cash's words.

"A bunch of people saw them out together after the game on Wednesday." Rachel studied his face and continued talking as if her question hadn't leveled him to the ground. "I kind of thought you and she were..."

"We're not."

"Okay." She shrugged. "See you later."

Then she flew back out the door with her sparkling dress, shimmering makeup and a piece of Cash's jaw.

Cash checked the clock for the thousandth time, but it was only five minutes later than the last time he'd checked: 7:55 p.m. The dance hadn't even started, and he was already agitated. Maybe he should go for a drive. He needed to keep his mind off what Rachel had said. Even if Olivia and Gil were dating, it was none of his business.

He picked up the phone and dialed Jack, surprised when his friend answered.

"Hey, aren't you at the dance tonight?"

"Nope. I'm on the couch supervising Tuck."

"How did you get out of chaperoning?"

"I paid attention in the staff meeting while Olivia was probably daydreaming about you. I had my excuses all lined up."

Cash imagined the middle part of that statement wasn't true. Wouldn't he know if Olivia was really dating Gil? Why wouldn't she have said something?

"So, what can I do for you?"

It took Cash a few seconds to register Jack's wry drawl. "Nothing."

"I'm glad we had this little chat."

Cash laughed and hung up.

Now what? It was 7:59. He strode over to the fridge and opened the door, scrounging for something. Nothing looked good. They were out of milk and bread. He could hit the grocery store. It would be dead on a Saturday night.

Grabbing his keys, he hopped in the truck, driving with the windows down and the country station cranked.

The H-E-B was as he'd expected. Cash grabbed a cart and rolled through the lanes, stocking up on frozen pizzas, pizza rolls, chips and any other man food he could find. In the cookie aisle he hit the jackpot with a couple packages of Double Stuf Oreos. He needed ice cream, too. The girls had demolished his mint chocolate chip stash.

By the time he got to the cash register, his cart looked as if a teenager had packed it. He went back and added a bunch of bananas and a bag of apples to even things out.

"Hello, Cash." Mrs. Brine greeted him at the checkout. The woman knew everything about every person in town—probably due to her job location and amazing sense of hearing. Whisper something across a room and Mrs. Brine would catch it.

"How are you tonight, Mrs. Brine?"

The woman blushed and clucked when he greeted her. "You'd best be saving those charms for someone younger. I hear you and Coach Grayson are on the outs."

Cash resisted the urge to growl. "We're not—" Forget it. It didn't matter what everyone thought. She finished ringing up his groceries, and he headed out to the truck. After throwing everything in the back, he jumped in and roared out of the lot.

What now? It was only a few minutes after nine. When the truck turned toward school like a horse with a mind of its own, Cash let it.

He parked at the back of the full lot, head falling to the steering wheel. What was wrong with him? He didn't need this. Didn't need to be checking up on Olivia like—

An ambulance siren blared and came closer, pulling into the lot and up to the front doors of the school. Cash hopped out, staying to the side as they rolled a stretcher in, knowing he needed to find his sister in order to calm the anxious blood roaring through his veins.

In the gym, Cash spotted Olivia and strode in her direction. He grabbed her arm and then winced when she jumped.

"Sorry. Didn't mean to shock you. Have you seen Rachel?"

Was that hurt on her face?

"Last I saw she was dancing with a group of her friends." Olivia scanned the crowd and pointed. "She's right there."

Cash found Rachel's light blond locks bouncing in time to the music. She laughed at something, her head tipped back with joy he hadn't seen in ages.

If she saw him, she'd lose that in an instant.

"Come on." He grabbed Olivia's hand, pulling her through the mass of students until they spilled out into the school entrance where the EMT helped a young girl onto a stretcher.

"Do you know what's going on out here?"

"I believe she had an allergic reaction to some of the food and she didn't have her EpiPen."

Cash stopped. Not only had he interrupted Olivia's evening, he'd acted like a bear. "Can you take a break?"

She looked at him as if he'd asked her to scoot the moon over a few inches. When Gil walked in their direction, Cash's shoulders tensed up into his neck.

"Hey, Gil." Olivia motioned to the outside doors. "I'm going to take a few minutes. I'll be back."

Gil waved. "Sounds good."

And that was that. The man kept walking toward the gym, not looking bothered in the least.

Cash and Olivia walked outside while Cash tried to calm his skittish pulse.

Now what?

They walked to his truck and he pulled the tailgate down. It seemed to be their place. After a second of analyzing, Olivia turned backward and lifted herself up. And that's when Cash lost his ability to speak for the second time in one evening. How had he not noticed what Olivia was wearing?

Her dress showed off her gorgeous legs and muscular arms, the perfect blend of mouthwatering and modest. The deep blue shimmered when she shifted on the tailgate, attempting to pull her skirt down. She was dressed like that and Cash offered her a truck tailgate to sit on?

Smooth move, Maddox.

Olivia's hair was pulled into some kind of messy knot at the back of her neck. Little wisps broke free and played in the evening breeze, dancing around her face. She had dangly earrings on and heels on her feet that probably made her the same height as him. Cash resisted the urge to pull her back down and see if their lips matched up.

"You look gorgeous."

Her eyes widened. "Thank you."

"I think you should wear that dress out to the ranch for tutoring next week."

She laughed and he scooted to a sitting position

on the tailgate next to her, trying for nonchalance. "So, what's new?"

Olivia looked over at him, amusement creasing the corners of her mouth.

"You pulled me out of a school dance to see what's new?"

Cash winced. He didn't even want to admit his real reason for being on school property to himself, let alone Olivia. His choices now seemed few.

Cut and run. Keep his mouth shut. Or lie.

And only two of those were possibilities.

Olivia wished she could read Cash's mind. He was acting crazy tonight.

"I'm sorry. I saw the ambulance and I freaked out."

Which still didn't explain why he'd been in the vicinity of the school in the first place. The man might be acting strange, but he still managed to turn heads. His simple white T-shirt molded over shoulder and arm muscles that made her feel a little crazy herself.

Resist, Liv. The man's not here for you. Then why was he here?

"Are you okay?"

"Yes." He let out a deep breath.

Olivia waited, letting the breeze cool her skin. The gym had been piping hot. She was ready to

be done with all of those dramatic hormonal teenagers, kick off her heels and drop onto her couch.

"So, anything new?" Cash reminded her of a
sprinkler, going over the same area again and again
and getting the same results.

"Nothing that I can think of." She'd just seen the
man on Thursday night. "Did I mention how great
your aunt and uncle are?"

Cash smiled for the first time, and Olivia's heart
plummeted. Gracious, he made her blood spin.

"You may have mentioned that, but I agree. They
are pretty great."

"Yep." Silence again. Olivia shifted, wondering
how she was going to climb down from the truck
tailgate and keep her skirt from riding up.

"I should probably go ba—"

"Are you dating Gil?"

"What?"

"Nothing."

Olivia's eyelids shuttered. "Am I dating Gil
Schmidt?" She opened her eyes to find Cash staring down at his hands. "No, I am not. But I did go
to dinner with him after the game on Wednesday."

"How come?"

"Because he asked and I was hungry."

Cash's gaze switched to her, his face broadcast-
ing feelings she didn't think she was supposed to

see. "I'm sorry. I know it's none of my business. You know this town and I just heard—"

"Don't you know not to believe everything you hear?"

At Olivia's teasing, Cash's lips barely curved. "Yes, ma'am. I do. I mean, I don't believe it. I just—" He slid a hand under the twisted hair at the back of Olivia's neck, pulling her forward until his forehead rested against hers. If not for her shallow breathing, Olivia would imagine her heart had just plain stopped.

When Cash pulled back just enough for his gaze to memorize her lips, Olivia shivered. "Don't."

A wounded look crossed his face, his hand dropping to his lap like a stone sinking to the bottom of a lake. Olivia snagged his hand and squeezed, wanting to erase that hurt.

"Rachel was so upset last weekend, and I think it was because your aunt was talking to me about you. I think she does need your full attention. It wasn't jealousy, but I'm not sure how to describe it."

She waited until those mesmerizing eyes clung to hers. "Don't go back on your promise." *Like I went back on mine.*

He traced a thumb along her cheekbone. "Liv." Cash's voice came across so soft and sweet, she'd never be able to resist if he offered another kiss.

Olivia hopped down from the truck and away from Cash's touch, feeling as though she'd ripped a Band-Aid off tender, burned skin. She adjusted the skirt of her dress and glanced at the building. "I should get back inside."

He jumped down too, only this time, he kept a foot of space between them. Good thing, since Olivia's resistance reserves had all gone into that one moment.

"I'm sorry about that." Cash rubbed the back of his neck, causing Olivia's nape to tingle with remorse at the absence of his touch. "You're right. I might not like it, but I know you're right."

Cash closed the tailgate, leaving his hands on it while his head tipped forward. Then he raised his jaw, determination traveling down his straightened back.

He faced her. "I'll walk you back inside."

"You don't need to." Her words were wasted. No matter how many times Olivia tried to refuse him, she knew he'd do exactly what he said. He was as sturdy as an oak. Completely dependable. Not the type of man to be anything but straightforward. If he had kissed her tonight, he would have been full of remorse. And then he would have backed away from her—maybe completely. It was better this way—with a barrier between them, with Rachel between them. By walking away from this moment, not only was Olivia helping Cash keep the promise he'd made, she was getting exactly what she wanted—enough distance to keep her heart from falling.

The thought couldn't be more disappointing.

Chapter Eleven

Cash watched Olivia as she carried a pitcher of sweet tea across Jack's parents' backyard. She was wearing a bright yellow sundress, and his mouth felt as though he hadn't had a sip of water in weeks. Though it wasn't the clothes that presented a problem. Olivia in tennis shoes and athletic gear gave him the same symptoms.

When she stopped to chat with Mrs. Smith, he forced himself to turn away. It had been three weeks since that moment at the homecoming dance. He and Olivia had gone back to friendship, neither of them mentioning the current that had flowed between them that night—and if he admitted it, ever since.

"Hello? Did you hear anything I just said?" Jack punched Cash on the arm, making the lemonade in his hand slosh over the rim of the red plastic cup and drip to the freshly cut grass beneath his tennis shoes. "You didn't, did you? I try to discuss football with my best friend and he can't stop drooling over the volleyball coach."

"Hey." Cash returned Jack's arm punch, making his tea slosh, too. "Keep it down."

The Smiths' backyard overflowed with parents, students, fall sports teams and anyone else who'd finagled an invite to Jack and Janie's annual mid-season party. They hosted it at Jack's parents' because the house and yard had way more room, but Janie and Jack did a majority of the preparation.

Jack shook the moisture from his hand. "I don't think there's a person here who doesn't know you have a thing for Olivia."

Cash groaned and his friend grinned.

"How many times do I have to tell you that it's not like that with us?"

"As many times as you look at her that way."

Cash adjusted the brim of his Billies baseball hat, thankful for the cover. This conversation was not what he needed right now. He didn't need any encouragement to think about Olivia.

"Hey, brother." His sister greeted him as she walked past with Val, giving him just the reminder he needed for why he had to resist the pull Olivia had on him. Rachel had improved so much over the last month, and Olivia had a lot to do with that. The girl talked more. She even smiled sometimes. And greeting him in public just now? She wouldn't have done that a few weeks ago. Rachel and Olivia had buddied up. When Olivia came out to the ranch on Thursdays, she and Rachel chatted the whole time they worked.

Cash watched his sister walk away with a mixture of joy and sadness in his gut. It seemed if he wanted the one to be happy, he couldn't have the other. He definitely did not want to mess with Rachel's improvement.

"Did you eat yet?" Jack asked.

"Nope. But I'm about to." The Smiths provided the meat, and everyone else chipped in with side dishes: plates of corn on the cob, homemade potato salad, green beans, pasta salad, spicy pinto beans, mashed potatoes and fried okra cascaded down the old picnic table like a wedding procession. Cash's mouth watered at the sight. The table's legs looked as though they might give out and sink into the green grass. And that didn't even include the separate table covered in pies, cobbler, brownies and cookies.

He and Jack went through the line, then carried their heaping plates to where Janie and Olivia sat in a circle of folding chairs.

Cash was surprised to see the two of them taking a break. He settled next to Olivia, realizing he'd missed her this week. She'd only skipped one Thursday to help Janie prep for the party, yet it felt like weeks since he'd talked to her.

"What's going on?"

She wiped her mouth with a napkin. "I'm exhausted. I didn't think there was much that could wear me out more than shopping with your sister for a day, but this takes the cake."

He answered her tired but beautiful smile with one of his own.

"What's going on with you?" she asked.

"I've just been roping and riding."

She laughed, then leaned closer. The movement caused her soft brown hair to swing in his direction. "How's the deal going with that grocery store in Austin?"

"Still haven't agreed on anything. They want me to come down so low that I'll barely make a profit."

A frown pulled on her lips. "I'll keep praying."

If his heart hitched a bit at her words, Cash ignored it. "Thanks."

"Olivia, I can't believe you didn't tell us," Janie interrupted, her voice full of accusation. "I had to find out from Facebook." She held up her phone, the Facebook app still open on the screen.

Olivia's eyes widened as she swallowed a bite of potato salad. "What?"

"Your birthday is next Saturday!"

"Oh, right." Olivia seemed relieved. Over what?

"We're definitely going out for Olivia's birthday, aren't we, boys?"

Jack and Cash agreed while Janie kept right on talking. "What should we do? I know—"

"Nothing. We don't need to do a thing."

"Now that's about the craziest thing I've ever heard. Don't y'all celebrate birthday week up in Colorado?"

"My wife seems to think the whole month of her birthday revolves around her."

Janie flashed her husband a scathing look. "I don't just think it. It does revolve around me."

They all laughed.

"Girl, you need to milk this thing."

Olivia stood. "I'm good, Janie. I promise."

Jack and Olivia went to throw their plates away, leaving Cash with Janie.

"We are so doing something for her."

Cash couldn't agree more. "Let me plan it."

The words must have surprised Janie as much as they surprised him, because she reeled back in her chair. Now that the idea had formed, Cash liked it.

"Trust me, Janie. I can handle this."

The lines on Janie's face softened. "Oh, Cash." She didn't have to say any more to communicate what she was thinking.

He stood and went to throw his plate away too. Cash might not be able to date Olivia or let his feelings progress beyond friendship, but he could plan something special for her birthday.

He could care *about* her…just not *for* her. There was a difference.

He hoped.

At five o'clock on Saturday evening, Olivia answered the knock on her apartment door to find a breathless Janie on her step.

"Happy birthday!" Janie brushed past Olivia and into her apartment, a bag over her shoulder and some kind of makeup kit in her hand. "Are we ready to get ready?"

Olivia glanced down at her favorite jeans and her new shirt. "I am ready."

Janie winked. "No, you're not."

"Wait. Where are we going? I thought we were going out to dinner?"

"That's part of it." Janie disappeared into Olivia's bedroom, then came back out, propping hands onto her slim hips. "What are you waiting for?"

To stop being confused.

Olivia followed Janie into her bedroom, only to find the blue dress she'd worn to homecoming pulled out of the back of her closet.

"What are you doing with that thing?"

"I'm about to wrestle it on your body. Cash said—" Janie pursed her lips. "Trust me. You need to wear this dress."

"But I'd look like an idiot going anywhere in this town dressed like that."

"Not…anywhere." Janie took the dress off the hanger while Olivia's mind raced.

"What are you wearing?"

Janie went over to Olivia's bed, grabbed the bag she'd been carrying and pulled out the dress she'd worn to her anniversary dinner. Flowing, strapless and soft pink, it easily compared in dressiness to Olivia's.

"I didn't think Bejas Grill had a dress code."

Janie laughed. "I can tell you we are definitely *not* going to Bejas Grill."

"Then where are we going?"

Janie tilted her head. "Sorry, girl. You won't get a thing out of me."

Olivia groaned. What choice did she have?

She put the dress on, wishing her heart would get excited about the evening. Her friends had planned a birthday night for her. Shouldn't she be happy about that? But she could only think about turning twenty-seven. This was definitely not where she'd expected to be at this point in her life. She'd always thought she would be married by this age. Maybe even expecting. Instead, thoughts of the past had plagued her all day like a coffee stain on her favorite white shirt. But tonight wasn't the time to process any of those. She'd been doing that for over a year and hadn't gotten much beyond anger and remorse. Surely she could take a night off.

Janie tugged Olivia into the bathroom. "Let's do our hair and makeup. It will be just like prom."

Janie's comment made Olivia laugh, and her tense body began to relax. What did she have to be upset about? Sure, she was about to spend the evening with a man who was becoming far more than a friend in her heart. But between their mutual commitment to Rachel and her inability to move beyond—or talk about—the past, their relationship would stay officially friend zoned.

According to Janie, birthdays were like free days. So Olivia would call in sick on all of her heartbreak and just enjoy herself for the evening.

A little fun couldn't hurt, could it?

"This is too much." Olivia sucked in a breath when they rounded the bend and the restaurant came into view. Cash did his best to keep his focus on the long drive instead of the stunning woman across the cab of the truck from him.

The Rose Hill Manor sign welcomed them, along with a two-story white building that boasted porches on both levels. Lights glowed from inside, illuminating the restaurant as dusk settled over the evening.

"Janie, I can't believe you did this." Olivia directed her comment to the backseat.

From the seat behind him, Janie nudged Cash

on the back of the head before answering Olivia. "It's a French menu tonight."

Thankfully Janie didn't finish the rest of that sentence: *and I didn't come up with it, Cash did.*

He didn't want Olivia to know that he'd planned the evening, because he didn't want to do anything to ignite the kindling that smoldered between them. Tonight was about making Olivia's birthday special. It had nothing to do with him, and everything to do with her.

Cash parked, and they all got out and walked up to check in with the maître d'.

"I do have your reservations and they're setting up your table now. Would you care to wait on the veranda for a few minutes?"

"Sure." Cash stepped away.

Janie announced she needed to use the restroom and Olivia agreed. They linked arms, heads tipped together as they walked down the hall.

Jack and Cash moved outside, and his friend sank into one of the wrought-iron chairs that lined the porch veranda. "Why do women always go to the bathroom together? What do they do in there?"

Cash took the seat next to Jack. "I don't have a clue."

"I think there's a TV in there playing sports."

His mouth hitched up. "I doubt that."

Jack pulled on the top button of his shirt. "I

thought Janie was going to make me wear a tie. I'm glad she stopped at the dress shirt."

Cash grinned and adjusted his dress pants—which he only wore to weddings and funerals—wishing for a pair of jeans right about now. Had he been wrong to plan all of this? Was it too much?

"They're ready to seat us." Olivia and Janie spilled outside, but Cash only had eyes for Liv. His memory of that dress did not do it—or her—justice.

He winced. Planning this evening might not have been his wisest move. But what could he do about that now? Even if he could escape the night, he didn't want to. And that concerned him even more.

"That was beyond delicious. Honey-lacquered duck, chestnut soup and then *mignardises*." Olivia let out a contented sigh as they walked outside and down the front steps of the restaurant. She hadn't eaten like that since her trip to France. It only made her want to go back and eat in tiny cafés and drink coffee near the Seine. All with the man next to her.

Oops. Scratch that last thought. Her plans for avoiding the past tonight should probably also exclude any thoughts of an unattainable future.

Enjoying the evening would work much better that way.

"No one has any idea what you just said or what we just ate."

Olivia rewarded Jack's comment with a punch on the arm.

How could she have dreaded this night? She couldn't ask for a better group of friends. Her stomach hurt from all the laughter during the meal. Jack and Cash had been comical when the amuse-bouche had arrived at the table. As if the whole meal consisted of those few small bites. She'd explained that it was something the chef thought would complement the meal and a small taste of what was to come. From then on, the evening had just gotten sillier. She couldn't remember when she'd had more fun.

They loaded in the truck and Cash drove back to Jack and Janie's house.

"Let's go change. I'm ready for the second half of my birthday night. I mean, Olivia's birthday night."

Janie's comment made them all laugh.

"Wait. There's more?"

"It's not as fancy." Cash answered Olivia and then cleared his throat. "Right, Janie?" He glanced in the rearview mirror.

"Right, Cash."

Her dry tone made Olivia's lips curve. What was going on between Janie and Cash tonight? Could

Janie be back to her matchmaking? Ever since the night Olivia had babysat Tucker and talked to Janie, her friend hadn't made any more attempts to push them together. At least, not that Olivia knew of.

When they got back to the Smiths', Olivia popped over to her apartment to change while the other three went to Jack and Janie's. She'd been told casual. Did that mean jeans or yoga pants? Cash had said something about outside, so Olivia opted for the jeans and shirt she'd been wearing earlier. Her hair and makeup looked silly with the casual outfit, but she just grinned at the bright-eyed girl in the mirror.

The sound of Tucker's screams greeted her on the sidewalk as she walked back to the Smiths'. After knocking on the glass door, she let herself in, finding everyone gathered in the small kitchen.

"He's been like this all night off and on." Jack's mom ran frustrated fingers through her hair. "I'd distract him and then all of a sudden he'd get upset again."

Janie held Tucker to her shoulder, soothing him while she comforted Jack's mom at the same time. "It sounds like an ear infection to me." She ran a hand over Tucker's forehead as his eyelids drooped. "He was like this when he had one before. Jack, can you get the ibuprofen?"

Jack rummaged through the cupboards, then slipped the dropper into Tucker's mouth. The tired boy took the dose without complaint.

"I'll rock him for a bit." Janie looked to Olivia. "Can you help me?"

"Sure." Olivia followed Janie into Tucker's room and took the stack of folded clothes off the rocking chair so Janie could sit.

"Thanks. Could you put those on the dresser? I didn't get them put away before we left."

Olivia did while Janie set the chair in motion.

"I'm sorry for ruining your birthday."

Olivia smoothed a hand across Tucker's dinosaur footie pajamas at the top of the pile, mouth curving up. "I am pretty upset with you."

Janie laughed, but Tucker didn't move from his cuddled position against her shoulder. He'd popped a thumb into his mouth, and with each slide of the chair, his eyelids drooped a little more.

"You and Cash go on and finish the rest of the night. There's no reason for the evening to end. I'll put Tucker to sleep, and the medicine will kick in. In the morning I'll call Dr. Hoke and get a prescription." Janie smiled over the top of Tucker's head. "Sometimes it pays to be a nurse."

"How long will it take for him to feel better?"

"Probably by Monday. But if not, I can always

call in sick. I…haven't been feeling great, so I wouldn't mind a day off."

Janie had been sick? When had Olivia missed this?

"I didn't know you weren't feeling well. Why didn't you say anything?"

Even in the soft light coming through the blinds, Olivia could see Janie's smile grow. "We haven't told anyone yet."

Olivia let out a squeak that made Tucker shift. "You're pregnant?" she whispered, but her excitement still came through.

Janie nodded. "We haven't even told our parents yet, so mum's the word. I'm only a few weeks along."

"Your secret is safe with me." Olivia checked her gut, surprised to find only warmth there instead of regret. She couldn't be happier for Janie and Jack. They were exactly the kind of parents who should keep right on having kids and filling up a whole house.

"So, go. Shoo. Have fun."

"How's Cash even going to know what the next plan is? I mean, weren't you in charge?"

"I'll only say this. I don't know the plan." Janie laughed softly. "Think about tonight and take a guess. That's all I'm going to say."

That made absolutely no sense. If Janie hadn't planned the evening, then…?

Cash.

The thought made Olivia's limbs feel the consistency of yogurt.

"Why would he do that?" Her whisper came out strangled.

"Oh, Liv, don't you know?"

"Janie, I can't—" Olivia would not go into her own issues right now. "He doesn't want to date because he wants to give Rachel his undivided attention."

Janie's sigh filled the room. "I've always wondered about that."

"I respect his decision, and I'm trying to be supportive of that. Rachel even seems to be getting better. I don't think she wants us dating either." Not to mention all of Olivia's reasons for staying detached. She moaned. "What am I supposed to do now?"

Janie got up and put Tucker in the crib, then waited to make sure he stayed sleeping. She walked over, placing her hands on Olivia's arms.

"I wish I knew, honey. I wish I knew."

Chapter Twelve

Cash opened the passenger door for Olivia, then went around to his side and got in. Jack and Janie had insisted he and Olivia finish her birthday evening without them. Which meant Cash was headed out to spend the rest of the night alone with Olivia on something that closely resembled a date.

He winced at the word. The promise he'd made in regards to raising Rachel seemed to be working. She improved day by day, and Cash didn't want to do anything to mess with that.

The whole point of the evening was to celebrate Olivia's birthday and make the night special. He could still manage that, couldn't he? He'd just have to remember that the girl across the cab from him was off-limits. For more than just tonight.

Cash pulled the truck away from the curb and glanced over at Olivia. She studied his hands, and Cash looked down to see his knuckles turning white. He loosened his grip on the steering wheel and flexed his fingers, willing himself to relax.

"Do I get to know where we're going this time?"

The question made him grin. "Nope. Just sit there and look pretty."

She laughed, easing a bit of the tension that filled the truck. Cash drove to the edge of town and then turned off onto a long, narrow dirt road. He could practically feel Olivia's curiosity boiling.

"Cash Maddox, I am not going night fishing."

His lips twitched. "Not it."

"Or for a walk in a field in the middle of the night."

He laughed and Olivia whacked him on the arm. Good. Let them get back to friendship instead of the limbo of attraction they seemed to dance around.

They pulled through the trees, revealing row upon row of vehicles surrounding a huge white barn.

"What?" Olivia leaned forward, hands on the dash. "Is that a movie?"

"Yep."

"That's so great. Whose place is this?"

"Gabe and Marcy Rowl's. On Saturday nights in the summer, they play a movie on the side of their barn. It's quite the attraction, but not everyone gets an invite."

"Really?"

"Not really, city girl. Anyone can come as long as they pay."

He received another jab to the arm.

Cash paid out the window, found a spot, put the truck in reverse and then backed in. He hopped out and met Olivia at the tailgate. Cash situated the mess of blankets and pillows he'd thrown in until it looked semicomfortable. They both climbed in and Olivia sat back, straight into Cash's shoulder.

"Oops. Sorry." She scooted over a few inches, then leaned back again. "It's about to start."

"Yeah, the stuff with Tuck put us a bit behind. I wish he felt better."

"Me, too."

Their voices turned to whispers as the music started, making everything feel even more intimate. Cash glanced around at all of the other cars, reminding himself that he and Olivia weren't alone. It just felt like it.

"Oh, my." Olivia's arms flapped. "Did you—? How did—?"

She looked as though she might hyperventilate.

"What?" Cash grabbed her arm, trying to calm her with a firm touch. "What's wrong?"

She turned to him with tear-filled eyes, making his chest ache. What could possibly be wrong?

"It's my movie. It's *You've Got Mail*."

He'd forgotten about that part. Amazing what a

couple pounds of ribs could get a person. But the way Olivia was looking at him… "Stinking Janie."

Olivia bit her lip. "She didn't *exactly* tell me you planned the night. I sort of guessed."

She leaned close, looking as if she might press a kiss to his cheek. When she shifted back, Cash resisted the urge to haul her into his arms and never let go.

"Thank you. This is the sweetest thing anyone has ever done for me. Cash Maddox, you are the most irresistible—"

"Stop," he growled. "Don't tempt me, woman." He sat back against the truck, crossing his arms to keep from reaching for Olivia. Continuing this night had not been the best idea.

Halfway through the movie, Olivia shifted. Between the smell of her shampoo and the few inches closer to him she'd ended up…for pity's sake. He needed to get a handle on his emotions.

She moved again, and he bit back his amusement. "You comfortable?"

"I'm good." When she tipped her head back to smile at him, Cash's attention focused on a tempting place to land a kiss. Definitely *not* good.

His phone buzzed in his pocket but he ignored it, stuck in the moment with Olivia. When it quit and started again, Cash shifted so that he could dig it out. Olivia moved to the side, and the connection between them thankfully ebbed.

Unknown Number flashed on his phone. "I'm going to take this in the cab," he whispered to Olivia, then accepted the call so that he wouldn't lose it. After climbing inside and shutting the door, he spoke.

"This is Cash."

"Cash." The voice that answered made his blood chill. "This is Sheriff Winston."

When Cash got into the truck cab, Olivia shifted a few inches away from where he'd been sitting. Janie-land birthdays might not have rules, but Olivia's heart felt too tender for that.

The man had made a promise, and Olivia wanted to help him keep that promise. And although her attraction to him seemed to grow every day—despite her demanding it not to—she still didn't feel the freedom to let her heart go. When tempted to give in to her feelings for Cash, Olivia only needed to remember the night when she had agreed with him about waiting for marriage and hadn't told him about Josh or the baby. It made fear trickle through her limbs to think of telling him now. Would he consider her part of that conversation a lie?

She tried not to think about the answer to that question.

Cash appeared beside the bed of the truck, but instead of climbing in, he motioned for her to come closer. "We have to go. Rachel's in jail."

His whisper froze Olivia in place. No. Impossible. "But she's been—"

"So much better. I know." At Cash's dejected sigh, she pushed all of the blankets and pillows to the front of the truck bed and then jumped down from the tailgate.

Cash met her at the passenger door. "Is she injured?"

"No. She's fine." When he opened her door, Olivia climbed inside, pulse slowing a bit. As long as Rachel was safe, they would handle whatever had happened.

Oh, Liv. She sounded as though she was part of this family. But she wasn't.

Cash got into the cab and pulled out without lights until they were far enough from the movie not to disturb the others.

It took him a few miles to speak. "She lied to me."

Olivia sucked in a breath. The quietly spoken words twisted like a knife in her own conscience.

"She told me she was spending the night at Val's. Instead, she went to a party with Blake and a bunch of other kids. Val wasn't even there. They never even had plans." Cash's hands clenched the wheel, then released. "They were drinking. She got into a car with a drunk driver. Renner." The way Cash said the boy's name sent chills down Olivia's spine. "I need to go pick her up. They're not holding her. They're letting the kids who weren't driving go home."

Olivia reached across the space and squeezed his arm, knowing no words would comfort Cash right now. Rachel could have been killed. All of the kids could have been killed.

When Cash pulled up in front of Olivia's apartment, they both spoke at the same time.

"Thanks—"

"I'm sorry—"

Olivia attempted a smile. "Thank you for tonight."

Cash tugged on his shirt collar. "I'm sorry your birthday night was ruined."

"It wasn't. It was perfect." Olivia paused, weighing her next words. "Do you…want me to go with you to get Rachel?"

"I'll handle it, but thank you for offering."

"Sure." Olivia hopped out of the truck, and Cash started to open his door. "Cash, you don't need to walk me up. Just go."

"No." His wooden tone made her cringe. He got out and slammed his door, meeting her in front of the headlights. "She needs to stew in there a bit. Isn't that what you told me after Rachel climbed on the church roof?"

Storm clouds of frustration and worry rolled across Cash's face, making Olivia's heartbeats slow with dread. How could she help?

They walked up the wooden steps, and after unlocking her apartment door, Olivia turned and slipped her arms around Cash's waist. Gone was the chemistry between them from earlier. Now she just wanted to comfort.

Cash hugged her back, but after a minute, he loosened his hold. "I better go."

Dejection weighed down his shoulders as he walked down the stairs. When the truck pulled away, Olivia started to pray.

She might be able to award herself a few points for enjoying the night and not letting the past torment her, but on thoughts of the future, her score would be a whopping negative twenty. Because what she felt right now about Rachel and Cash was nowhere near as removed as it needed to be.

Even the coffee mug steaming in Olivia's hand didn't make the morning better. Everyone at the Monday morning staff meeting seemed to be functioning in silent mode because of Saturday night's trouble.

Gil took the chair next to her, then leaned close. "How are you holding up?"

She wobbled her hand in answer, trying not to trigger new tears. She'd done enough of that yesterday and a bucketful of praying, too. God could handle this. He had a plan for Rachel, even if Olivia couldn't see it.

When the principal entered the room and strode to the front of the long table the teachers sat at, Olivia's back straightened. She loved Mrs. Dain. The woman ran a good school, but this morning Olivia felt as if she was about to be sentenced for a crime. Or at least a few students were.

Jack looked at her from across the table, a silent understanding passing between them. His star running back had been driving. How much worse would all of this be for Blake?

Mrs. Dain filled the staff in on some of the details. A trooper out on Route 16 had seen the car leave a party and pulled the teens over before they could cause harm to anyone else. Blake had been charged with a DUI, while the passengers had been questioned and released without charges.

"Each of the students involved will be suspended for a week of school. Passengers are not eligible to play sports for two weeks."

No. Olivia glanced down, pretending to find interest in the papers in front of her. Rachel wouldn't be allowed to play right up to the state tournament. They only had two more matches, one of which they needed to win in order to even make it to state. Now her star hitter and blocker—and a young girl she cared very much about—would miss those games. Olivia had two practices to find a replacement for Rachel.

"And the driver, Blake, is not eligible to play sports for the rest of the year."

That statement sucked the air out of the room.

Mrs. Dain finished up with a few more announcements and dismissed the staff. Olivia sat at the table, stunned. Her heart ached for Rachel. The girl had a chance for a college scholarship. They'd worked so hard on bringing her grades up, and for what? For her to possibly throw that chance away.

What must Cash be feeling and thinking? If Olivia was this upset, he'd be tormented. And blaming himself.

Jack slipped into the vacated chair next to Olivia. "How is he?"

"When he dropped me off...I've never seen him like that. Angry, brooding. Kind of a deadly storm."

"Figured."

"What are you going to do without Blake?"

Jack's shoulders hitched. "Play football. Is your team going to be okay without Rachel?"

Olivia released a slow breath. "We're going to have to be."

Olivia shifted both bags to her left hand and knocked on the Maddoxes' front door, hoping she was doing the right thing. It had been a long week, and she imagined that Cash and Rachel could use some support. Last night's match had been rough. The team had been off their game without Rachel, their emotions on edge. Megan, a sophomore, had played in Rachel's spot. She'd done an exceptional job for being thrown into the position, but she just didn't compare to Rachel. Though they'd made a team effort, it hadn't been enough for a win.

Next week's game would dictate whether the team made it to the state tournament or if the season was over. If they did win, Rachel would be eligible to play just in time.

Olivia knocked again.

Cash answered the door wearing a white UT T-shirt and faded jeans. Despite the awful situation with Rachel and the weathered lines pulling down the corners of his mouth, the man still made her pulse jump-rope.

"Hey. What are you doing here?"

Olivia stepped inside, set the food and schoolwork bag on the floor and walked into Cash's arms. A deep shudder ricocheted through his chest as his arms came around her. He reminded her of a balloon with a pinhole in it, the air slowly leaking out of him.

After a minute he stepped back and squeezed her arms. "Thanks. I needed that." He grabbed her stuff from the floor, putting both bags on the table. "What's all this?"

"Dinner." She pointed to the Chinese takeout. "And I got all of Rachel's schoolwork from her teachers."

"Thank you. You didn't need to do all of that."

"I wanted to. So, where's the prisoner?"

Cash's grin gained a bit of traction before it faded. "Up in her room."

"I see the house looks perfectly clean."

"The house, laundry, mucking out stalls and anything else I can think of."

Cash moved to the front of the couch and collapsed onto the cushions. Olivia followed, sitting next to him and facing his profile.

She waited, knowing he needed to talk—even if he didn't know it.

Finally, he turned his dejected face in her direction. "I don't know what to do with her. I thought she was getting better and opening up. Her grades were improving." He let out a shuddering breath, looking far older than his twenty-seven years. "And now this… I don't think she realizes how serious this is, how bad it could have been." Stress lines cut through his forehead. "And on top of that, she did the one thing I asked her not to do. She lied."

Olivia nibbled on her lip, trying to ignore her own sense of panic and concentrate on Rachel. "She is a teenager. They make mistakes and—"

"So?" Cash shook his head. "It doesn't matter how old she is. How am I supposed to trust her again?" His sigh shook the couch. "I'm not sure how to protect her. I'm thinking about sending her to live with Uncle Dean and Aunt Libby." He looked as though someone had snuffed out his faith, his hope.

"Have you talked to them about it? What did they say?"

"They said they'll support us just like they've always done. They want to take some time for all of us to pray about it. So that's what we're doing."

"Does Rachel know?"

Cash slowly shook his head.

The magnitude of the discussion filled the first floor of the house. If Olivia felt as if she was drowning, what must Cash feel like? Did he expect her to have answers? She'd come here to be a support, but she didn't know how to help with this. "I don't know what to say."

Cash's shoulders fell.

"But I can pray."

He managed a sad smile. "We'll take all the prayers we can get."

Chapter Thirteen

The bell rang and students flew from Olivia's classroom as if she'd given them a pop quiz. Which she had. She stacked the papers thrown onto her desk, then slipped them into her bag to take home.

"Coach Grayson?"

Olivia looked up to see Rachel standing in her classroom doorway. She played with her hair and looked everywhere but at Olivia.

"Hey, come on in."

"I know you need to get to practice." Rachel walked into the room and took a seat across from Olivia.

"I have a few minutes. What's up?"

"I finished my work for the week, so I wanted to let you know that you don't have to come out to help me tonight."

Olivia had to remind herself that was a good thing. She hadn't seen Cash since last Thursday at the ranch, but he had texted her before the game last night to say he was praying for her. Bless that man. She'd needed it. The girls had needed it, too. But they'd rallied, winning in five games without their star player. Olivia already felt the anticipation of Rachel coming back and having her team all together again. Maybe the girls felt it too.

"I'm so glad you won last night." Rachel echoed Olivia's thoughts and then swiped under her eyes.

Was she crying?

Olivia grabbed the tissue box and moved to the chair next to Rachel, setting the box on her desk.

"When I think about how I almost ruined our chance to go to state…" Moisture spilled onto her cheeks, and Olivia reached across to squeeze her hand.

"But you didn't. We made it."

"I'm sorry." Rachel sniffed, taking a tissue to wipe her cheeks and blow her nose. "I'm sorry for drinking and making things hard on the team. I'm sorry I was such a jerk to you in the beginning."

"I forgive you, Rach. You're young, and now you've learned a lesson that could change the rest of your life. Take it and run. Don't let the past weigh you down."

Wise advice. Maybe Olivia should try following it herself.

Rachel hooked hair behind her ear with a trembling hand. "I just wish…"

When she didn't continue, Olivia prompted her. "Wish what?"

"It's stupid."

"I'm all about stupid. Bring it on."

Rachel laughed and glanced to the side. "Blake's been such a jerk since that night."

Olivia's breath stuttered along with her pulse. "Rachel, he's never...he wouldn't hurt you, would he?"

Rachel's head swung back and forth. "No. It's not like that. It's just that he's been in such a horrible mood since he was cut from the team. He's been ranting and raving about losing his chance for a scholarship and how the school's punishment was far too severe."

"The school has a zero-tolerance policy for drinking and driving. It's not like they singled him out."

"I know. Plus, he made the decision. No one forced him to drink and drive, just like no one forced the rest of us to get into the car."

Olivia felt a rush of pride at Rachel taking responsibility for her own decisions. The girl had changed in the few months since school had started—no matter what Cash thought. Was he still thinking of sending her to Austin? Olivia had tried to pray with an open mind over the last week, but deep in her heart, she didn't want Rachel to go.

And it had nothing to do with volleyball and everything to do with two people she cared deeply about.

"I kind of want to break up with Blake."

Rachel's whispered confession almost shocked Olivia out of her seat, but she forced herself to remain calm and wipe any surprise from her features.

"Then why don't you?" Cash would throw a parade. But Olivia didn't want to let his opinion taint hers, so she prayed for wisdom and waited for Rachel to speak.

The girl watched her hands as they twisted on the desk. "I don't know. I guess because I was with him and made the same choice."

"Not the same choice. You didn't drive. And even though you did get into the car, you've changed, Rachel—in a good way. Not just in the last two weeks, but in the last few months."

I hope these are Your words, Lord. Olivia surged ahead. "You don't have to stay in the same relationship and suffer because of one bad decision. You're in high school, not married to the boy."

That earned a laugh from Rachel.

"Take a break from him, or from anyone. High school's a great time to hang out with friends. You don't need a boyfriend to have fun."

"*Fun* is not the word I would use to describe Blake lately." Rachel stood. "You'd better get to practice."

Olivia stood and hugged her, and then Rachel

walked to the door and paused. "Can I come back to practice on Monday?"

A smile lifted Olivia's lips. "If you don't, I'm sending the whole team to track you down and drag you in."

The crowd roared around Olivia as the football team ran onto the field Friday night. She stood with Gil and a few other teachers, the stands rumbling under her blue tennis shoes. Tonight's conference football game would impact the team's standing and chance for making the state tournament in December. Hopefully they could win without Blake like they did last week.

Where was Janie? Olivia slipped her hands into the back pockets of her jeans and scanned the crowd. She hadn't heard much from her friend this week, but Janie would never miss a game.

Olivia turned back to the field to find Jack motioning to her from his sideline perch. She scooted along the row and jogged down the bleachers.

Jack met her at the edge of the grass, his face crowded with worry lines. "I can't get a hold of Janie. The baby—" He glanced down, cleared his throat. "She started spotting a few days ago and…"

"No." Olivia whispered the word, pain filling every fiber of her body. "Why didn't she call me?"

"Janie's tougher than she lets on and when she's in pain—" Jack scraped a hand across his chin.

"She doesn't want anyone around. I told her to call you. She said she would after…" His Adam's apple bobbed. "She took the day off and Tucker went to day care, but our day care called and left me a couple of messages saying that Janie never picked up Tucker. I didn't see the missed calls until a few minutes ago. I talked to my parents, and they're heading over to get Tuck, but I need someone to check on Janie while they're getting him. Her parents are driving back from San Antonio right now, so they can't, and—"

"I'll go check on her. Don't worry. I'm sure she's just sleeping." Olivia struggled to believe her own words.

Jack's stance relaxed, but he still scanned the stands as though Janie might appear at any moment. "Thanks. I really appreciate it."

"I'll text you when I get there, so check your phone."

Jack nodded.

"And go win a football game."

He barely managed a smile.

"Janie?" Olivia knocked for the second time on the Smiths' door, heart hammering.

I'm going to feel so horrible for waking her up if she's sleeping.

When no one answered, she opened the storm door and tried the knob. It turned under her hand,

and she stepped inside, pausing on the cheerful welcome mat. A moan came from the couch, and Olivia hurried around the front, finding her friend curled up in a ball, robe on with pajamas poking out.

"Janie?"

At her whisper, Janie opened groggy eyes. Olivia shuddered with relief, dropping to her knees. "You scared us half to death. I'm sorry I woke you up. We couldn't get a hold of you."

The horror of her friend's suffering caused the past to rear up. Olivia's mouth tasted like metal, and her legs felt as though they were made of lead. She sank from her knees to a sitting position on the hardwood floor.

"Sorry." Janie mumbled the word, eyelids drooping. Perspiration beaded her forehead, and her skin looked as if she hadn't seen the sun in years.

Olivia touched her wrist, shocked by the heat and erratic pulse.

"How long have you felt like this?"

"Last night and today." Janie took a shaky breath. "Did Jack tell you?"

Olivia nodded, tears pooling. "I'm so sorry. I feel so awful—"

Janie moaned and gripped her abdomen, then vomited into a bucket she had by the side of the couch.

Hands trembling, Olivia pulled out her cell and

dialed 9-1-1. She might be overthinking. It could be a common flu or something simple, but her gut didn't agree with that assessment.

She only knew her miscarriage had been nothing like this.

"What happened?" Jack flew into the waiting room, still in his red team polo and khakis, eyes wild with fear.

Olivia popped up. "I told you not to leave the game. The doctor said—"

"I don't care about a stupid football game!" Agitation came off Jack in waves.

"She's okay." Olivia rushed to reassure him, hoping she was right. "They said her miscarriage went septic and—"

"Septic? What does that mean?"

"It's an infection in the uterus. She was running a fever. They're putting her on antibiotics, and they rushed her in for surgery." Olivia paused, searching for the right words and swallowing over the sawdust in her mouth. "They need to make sure there's nothing left to cause the infection."

"You mean no part of the baby."

Jack's painful words, spoken so softly, shot straight into Olivia's soul. She wanted to find the nearest trash can and be sick.

"Did they say anything else about Janie?" Hope and fear mingled in Jack's expression.

"They just said what they needed to do, they didn't say—" They didn't say if her friend's life was in danger, but from what Olivia had seen on that couch…

Jack crumpled into a chair.

"I'm sure she's going to be fine, Jack. She's in great hands and we got here in time. They said it was good we didn't wait any longer."

He groaned. "I should have made her go in this morning when she was throwing up, but she's so stubborn. She said it was normal, that she would be fine. How do you argue with a headstrong nurse?" He dropped his head into his hands.

"I wouldn't have known either." Jack's dejected state made her feel helpless.

"Mr. Smith?" The doctor Olivia had seen earlier stood in the doorway, dressed in blue scrubs, his surgery mask pulled down around his neck.

Olivia tried to read his gaze, but she couldn't decipher a thing. The man must be practiced in the art of dealing with family—with good or bad news.

Jack popped up from the chair and braced himself in front of the doctor. "Yes, that's me."

"The surgery went well, but we need to monitor your wife to make sure she fights this infection. She's in the recovery room. You can see her now if you want to, but she's still pretty groggy."

"I want to see her." Jack choked over the words and then followed the doctor out of the room, leaving Olivia to drop into a chair. The trembling started in her legs, then moved to the rest of her body. Janie could have died today, and she wasn't in the clear yet.

Olivia held her head in her hands and prayed, for minutes or hours, she didn't know. Someone grabbed her hands and pulled her up. Her eyes flew open in time to see Cash's dusty shirt before he crushed her against his chest.

She leaned into him, soaking in all of his strength and warmth, letting it fill all the hollow places while tears streamed down her face. She didn't know how long she cried, just that Cash held her, rubbing her back. Finally her body shuddered and she felt the semblance of control coming back. What an outburst. And the man holding her didn't even know why. He thought all of it had to do with Janie—and most of it did—but he didn't know that part of it had to do with reliving the worst time of her life.

"I'm sorry."

Cash pulled back enough to retrieve a bandanna from his pocket. "You have nothing to apologize for." He wiped her face, then held it against her nose. "Blow."

She laughed through the tears. "I'm not blowing my nose with you holding it." She took the bandanna and then did as he said, stuffing it into her jeans pocket to clean later.

The tender way he looked at her…she just about crumbled again.

"How's Janie?"

Olivia filled him in on what little she knew.

After listening, Cash pulled her over to the chairs. He sank into one, tugging her into the one next to him.

The sleeves to his blue-and-green plaid work shirt were rolled up halfway between his wrist and elbow, and he brushed a hand across his chest. "Sorry. I may have mussed you up. I was out on the ranch when I heard and I'm a stinky, dusty mess."

"I may have added some snot to your shirt, so we're even."

He smiled, but the dark smudges under his eyes and the stubble on his cheeks made him look worn. The man took his responsibility for Rachel and the ranch very seriously, and Olivia worried about him.

"You've been working too hard again, buckaroo."

The lines around Cash's eyes crinkled. "I can handle it. I'm tough."

True. Sometimes too tough.

"Are you okay now?" He motioned to her tear-stained face. "Is this just about Janie or something else?"

The whisper in the back of her mind told her if she kept the past buried, it wouldn't define her. But her soul told a different story. She needed to tell him. But the question she'd been asking herself for months weighed down on her chest, stealing her breath.

Would he think she'd lied to him? And if yes, would he ever forgive her? Based on the way he'd reacted to Tera's and Rachel's lies, Olivia didn't hold out much hope. But despite the fact that she knew not telling Cash now would be a blatant lie and only make things worse, she couldn't force the words out.

What if she told him about Josh and he walked away?

She couldn't handle that kind of hurt on top of today's horrible memories. Her conscience screamed, trying to drown out the fear. *Just tell him the truth. Rip off the Band-Aid.*

"I—" She swallowed. "Just Janie." The words slipped out before Olivia could stop them, and she gripped the arms of her chair to keep herself upright.

Janie's parents clattered into the room and Cash stood, greeting them with hugs. Olivia popped up too, but couldn't move, couldn't join them. As Cash shared the medical updates with Janie's parents, Olivia's heart unraveled at the lie she'd just told. Why hadn't she told him the truth? Why couldn't she move past this?

She knew all of the right answers, knew that God wiped everything clean, yet she couldn't forgive herself for making a foolish mistake. Especially since she'd known better. And now, added to it, she'd hidden it from Cash. She felt sick, just like she had when she'd first arrived at the hospital.

Olivia hadn't thought it possible for her to actually make this situation worse, but she'd managed to accomplish exactly that. Now, not only did the past hold her captive, the future did too. Because she'd just lied to a man who would never forgive her.

Jack returned to the waiting room and everyone launched questions at him at once. He waved his arms to silence them. "She's awake and her fever is coming down with the medication. The doctor says as long as her body continues to fight the infection, she'll be okay."

Cash pulled Olivia close, tucking her into his shoulder. She closed her eyes, guilt slithering through her even as relief over Janie flooded her body.

"What did she say?" Janie's mom asked, wiping tears.

Jack scrubbed hands over his face and looked at the floor, obviously fighting emotion. Finally, he cleared his throat while everyone in the room wiped moisture from their eyes. "She cried. And then she asked me if we won the football game."

"You did." Janie's dad gripped Jack's shoulder. "We heard it on the drive over."

Janie's words gave Olivia a glimmer of hope that, with time, her friend would heal.

If only she still had that same verdict for herself.

Chapter Fourteen

Olivia and her team strode into the Strahan Coliseum for the state volleyball tournament, its maroon-and-yellow seats stretching end to end. A handful of other volleyball teams was spread through the stands or warming up on the court.

The nerves the girls had subdued on the almost two-hour bus ride to San Marcos seemed to swell with the size of the place.

Olivia checked in with the host to find out which locker room would temporarily be theirs. She sent the girls to change, then scanned the stands. The team had left early enough to watch the game before theirs, so only one or two sets of parents were in the stands. Olivia imagined that would change in the next hour or so. She'd even heard the football team talk about caravanning down together.

Janie wasn't up to traveling yet. She'd only spent one night in the hospital, but the infection had definitely drained her. Although she claimed to be feeling much better, a veil of pain was still visible in her eyes. And as Olivia knew from experience, that hurt would far outlast the physical.

In a red Billies coaching polo that matched Olivia's, Trish beckoned from the stands where she'd staked out a few rows. Olivia went up to meet her, and when the girls came out of the locker room, she and Trish waved them up. They lounged in the yellow chairs, legs draped every which way like only teenagers could do. Rachel had her iPod on, earbuds in, but she watched the game like everyone else. After watching each team win one game, Olivia motioned for her team to follow.

"Let's head over to the warm-up gym."

They walked over and she had the girls circle up, thankful they had the space to themselves. "I'm going to teach you a calming technique. Stick your stomachs out like this." She pushed her own out as an example. "Pretend you're filling up your stomach with air. Then when it feels like you're going to burst, let it out. Do that a couple of times."

Olivia winked at Trish, who turned the other way to hide her amusement. The girls followed her directions, some laughing when they couldn't hold the air any longer, others taking everything seriously.

"Coach, what is this supposed to do?" Val

paused, stomach out, words strained because of the position she was trying to hold.

"Nothing." Olivia smiled. "You guys look hilarious. You really shouldn't do everything your coach says."

Val's air came out in a whoosh and the other girls followed suit, everyone howling with complaints and laughter. Olivia's shoulders relaxed when the tension seeped away from her team. They grabbed balls and started warming up, laughing and talking like they would back at their home gym. Exactly what Olivia wanted. She'd seen plenty of teams lose because of nerves.

When they went back to the main gym for their first match, Cash, Libby and Dean waved down at her from the stands. Olivia waved back, then turned her attention to the game. She'd told her girls absolutely no thinking about boys today. Surely the rule applied to her also. And after what she'd said to Cash at the hospital, it was one she would gladly follow.

They'd won the first match and lost the second, but Olivia couldn't be more proud. The girls had played so hard in that second match. Now, the team they'd lost to was headed for the first-place game while the Billies played for third.

Hopefully her team could rally and regain their

momentum. A third-place trophy for the case at school would be nice.

The girls rounded up, stretching in the warm-up gym again. The tournament ran matches two out of three instead of three out of five like the normal season, but the team was still tired. Olivia felt time run together as the team gathered and ran out onto the main court. Trish talked to her, but Olivia couldn't focus on anything but the next match.

They won the coin toss and Olivia had Val serve. Her strong, consistent serve would set the tone for the game, much like Rachel's had done earlier.

Olivia didn't realize she was holding her breath until the opposing team's receive was already in the setter's hands. Three hitters approached the net, and the Billies' blockers moved to meet them. Unable to get a hand on the hit, the ball spun to the floor.

At the last second Mandy lunged and got an arm under the ball. It bounced off and back toward the far corner of the court. Since the setter couldn't get it, Bridget used a bump to get the ball as close to the hitter as possible.

While it was nowhere near a good set, Rachel stayed poised on the outside left as the ball came her direction. She timed her ascent perfectly and turned her shoulders, pulling the ball straight down the line and completely avoiding the blockers who'd been expecting a cross court hit.

The ball bounced near the line, and when the line judge's arms flew forward, Olivia's team let out a cheer.

Evenly matched, the two teams volleyed over and over again, making it look easy to receive each other's hits and serves. Seldom did a ball hit the court without someone getting a hand underneath it. They quickly flew through two games, coming up with a win for each.

When neither team pulled more than two points away from each other during the third game, Olivia thought her knees might give out. Instead of sitting, she stayed on the edge of the court, half wishing she could run out there and play with them but knowing they had the skills to do it themselves.

The ball ended up in the Billies' hands with one point needed to win. As Rachel tossed the ball up for her serve, Olivia pushed air in and out of her lungs and prayed.

Rachel's nerves must have kicked in, because the serve barely made it over the net. The other team easily received and bumped to their setter, who put up a quick middle hit. Billies blockers were in the wrong spot, leaving the back row to receive the strong hit.

Mandy rolled under the ball, her flat arm giving it an arc but pushing it too close to the net for an easy set. Sarah called out for a number-one play— a short set just above the net—and jumped up, setting the ball straight into Valerie's outstretched hand. The other team's blockers scrambled, but it was too late. The ball touched down, the smack vibrating through the momentarily quiet coliseum.

And then the screaming started. The girls pulled her onto the court, dragging Trish, too. Olivia tried to wrap her mind around the win as celebrating students and parents poured out of the stands and filled the court. Congratulations came from all sides.

Rachel stood in front of her, face filled with joy. "Thank you." She hugged Olivia and Olivia squeezed the girl in return. Rachel blinked back moisture before someone grabbed her from behind and hugged her. Olivia looked up to see Cash striding across the court toward her. Instead of waving or mouthing congratulations, he tore across the space and scooped her up in a massive hug. In that moment, all of the people faded away. Let the whole town think whatever they wanted. Olivia let herself enjoy the moment in Cash's arms, knowing it wouldn't last.

It was a good thing Libby hugged her next or she might have fallen over. "I'm so proud of you, Frenchie," Libby whispered in Olivia's ear. "Thanks for loving my niece and nephew. We'll see you at Thanksgiving."

It wasn't until after the crowds had thinned and she'd endured the long bus ride home that Olivia let herself dwell on Libby's comments. Her head sank into her soft pillow, but the words marched through her mind, keeping her awake.

Since Olivia didn't have a clue what Libby meant about Thanksgiving, she'd let that slide.

But the love thing?

Did she love Cash? Sure. She loved Rachel and Cash. But was she in love with Cash? Olivia didn't know. But…it was a possibility. And the fact that she could consider that question meant something had begun to change inside her. What if God had been answering her prayers about healing from the past, but she'd just been so wrapped up in her own guilt and inability to forgive that she hadn't noticed?

She'd thought at the hospital with Janie that she'd never move on, that her painful past would never heal, but now Olivia realized that wasn't true. She *had* begun to let go—even if it was just a little at a time. God had used Cash to answer a prayer for her. That place she'd thought might be broken forever…it had begun to mend under the steady attention of this man's friendship. Where there'd only been darkness, she now felt a warmth, a light shimmering. It felt like hope. The way Cash treated her made her feel of worth.

Olivia groaned, dropping an arm over her face. A small corner of her heart had begun to bloom again because of Cash, and she wanted to give him the same respect he gave her. Which meant she needed to tell him the truth. She'd kept it from him because…because she didn't want to lose that feeling, didn't want to lose him as a friend.

Not being honest with Cash at the hospital had been a mistake. But Olivia couldn't go down the path of self-loathing again. This time, she would claim God's forgiveness for this lie. And she would tell Cash the truth.

She climbed out of bed, dropping to her knees. A little girl again, she came to her Father for the grace He'd already offered. Undeserved grace and forgiveness waited for her. And this time she planned to figure out a way to take it.

Aunt Libby stifled a yawn as she poured two cups of decaf. Cash and Rachel were staying the night in Austin before heading home tomorrow in the hopes that Cash could figure out a plan for Rachel. Not knowing what to do left him feeling ragged at the end of each day.

Uncle Dean sat on the sofa in the living room, the TV on, his soft snores floating into the kitchen. Rachel had been exhausted from the tournament and had gone to bed.

Cash couldn't be more proud of how she'd played today. She'd seemed different since her night at the sheriff's office. Could they be getting somewhere with her? He didn't want to hope as he had so many times before. At least tonight he could talk to Libby about his concerns.

His aunt set a steaming blue mug in front of him along with the creamer. He added a bit and then stirred while she took a seat across from him.

The same eyes he'd inherited pinned him to the chair. "So, tell me what's on your mind."

"I don't know what to do with her, Lib. Every time she seems to improve, something pulls her back down. This last time, with the drinking, she could have been killed."

"I know, honey. Trust me, we pray over the girl all the time."

"She's doing better again, but I'm almost afraid to hope. I can't help wondering if she should come here and live with you."

"Why? What can we give her that you can't?"

"Maybe she'd be…safer." Emotion clogged his throat. "What if I mess up? What if she gets hurt? What if something happens to her like Mom and Dad?"

Libby wiped away tears that seemed to be constantly present. "Cash Maddox, you know you can't control something like that. No one gives and takes away life but God. Rachel would be no safer here than with you. And as for messing up, you're the complete opposite. You'd do anything for her. You go to all of her games, love her when she's a brat, ask Olivia to tutor her when she needs help with schoolwork." Libby snagged a napkin and blew her nose. "Dean and I have been praying about it like we said, but neither of us think Rachel's supposed to move here."

Cash didn't know if the settling in his shoulders was relief or pressure.

"If you really can't do it, you know we will. But what we see is different from what you see. Rachel's a normal teenager dealing with some horrible things life's thrown her way. She's not doing drugs. She goes to school and wins volleyball games." Libby slammed her palms against the table, causing Uncle Dean's snore to break into three jagged parts. "You're doing a great job. Stop punishing yourself."

He'd been praying for a clear answer, and it didn't get much more direct than that. Relief trickled down his spine. No matter how crazy Rachel drove him, no matter how much he worried about her, he didn't want to lose her.

"So, are you going to tell me what happened?"

Cash tilted his head. "With Rach? You know what happened."

"No, crazy. With the woman you look at like she can make your mom's lasagna, wrap it up in a bow and fly it over to you."

Cash considered pretending he didn't know who Libby was talking about. Why did everyone think it fair game to bring up this subject with him? "Nothing's happened. We're the same as we've always been. Friends."

Libby snorted and Dean's snore followed suit before settling back to a quieter version.

"I'm not sure who you watched more at the tournament today—your sister or Olivia."

He could admit to a few glances and one hug, but that was it. Nothing to blow out of proportion. And if he'd fought the feeling all day that he had two girls on that court instead of one, he certainly wouldn't be admitting it to Libby.

"I can't see anyone, you know that. Rachel needs all of my attention, now more than ever. I promised—"

"You promised what?"

"That I wouldn't date anyone or take my attention away from Rachel. You know that if I'd gone with Dad that day, Mom would still be alive. If I hadn't trusted Tera and gone over to check on her, then Rachel wouldn't be stuck with me—"

"That's a lot of *if*s." Libby squeezed his hand, coffee ignored. "I hear you that you made a promise, but let me tell you something. You *cannot* give Rachel the same childhood you had. She's never going to have the same life you did. You had your parents for longer than she did, and that is *not* your fault. Life isn't fair. You didn't cause that accident. Your mom isn't gone because of you. God obviously wanted you on this earth, and you're going to have to accept His plan." She waved a manicured hand, voice rising. "Do you control the universe? Give and take away life? Are you God?"

"Of course not."

"You're acting like it."

Cash opened his mouth to protest, but Libby barreled right on by.

"Have you even asked Rachel?"

"Asked her what?"

"What she thinks of you dating. You've been making this decision without her input, assuming you know what she needs. She'd probably pick Olivia over you."

Cash couldn't decide whether to laugh or be offended.

"You're lovesick, boy. Don't lose Olivia because you're trying to control everything."

Cash kneaded the back of his neck, not quite sure what to do with this barrage of information.

"Have you asked God about this promise of yours?" Libby's words cut to Cash's soul in a way nothing else had so far. "Is it something He asked you to do or did you come up with it all on your own?"

"I—" The words stopped as doubt held his tongue. He wanted to tell Libby that he'd only been following God's plan in regards to Rachel.

But for the first time in his life, he didn't know if it was the truth.

Chapter Fifteen

"I need to stop for gas." Cash glanced across the cab of the truck. Rachel didn't give any response, but who knew if she heard anything with those things in her ears.

After attending church this morning with Dean and Libby, they'd started back to Fredericksburg. Rachel had pretty much been glued to her phone or iPod, earbuds in the whole time, leaving Cash to sort through his skittish thoughts.

Libby's words had haunted him through much of the night, and now he couldn't stop yawning due to the lack of sleep.

Could Libby be right? Had he made up the promise because of his own desire for control?

Cash didn't know. He didn't know much of anything right now.

He didn't recall ever asking God, and he'd definitely never asked Rachel. But hadn't God given him the idea to make the promise in the first place? Where else would he come up with something like that?

Cash clicked through the stations until he found some country, but nothing calmed his mind. He could ask Rachel. She was sitting right next to him. Too bad he didn't know what to say.

At the next gas station, he pulled off to fill up. When he stopped, Rachel hopped out. Minutes later, she came back with a blue Gatorade in one hand and a coffee in the other.

"Thought you'd want a coffee since you can't stop yawning."

"Thanks." Surprised, Cash accepted the cup. His sister certainly had a sweet side...when she wanted to show it.

Rachel buckled up while he got back on Highway 290. When she didn't put her earbuds back in immediately, Cash's mind took off at speeds his horse would know well. Should he ask her about what Libby had said?

"Rach."

She glanced at him, fingers pausing from doing something on her phone. "Yeah?"

"You did great yesterday. I'm really proud of you."

She smiled, then glanced out her window. "Thanks."

"And I'm proud of you for how you acted these last few weeks after the..."

"The incident?"

"Is that what we're calling it now?"

"I'd rather not call it anything, but it did happen."

True. "Can I ask you a question?"

"Sure." Rachel stretched the word out, probably wondering why he was acting so strange.

"Have you ever noticed that I don't date anyone?"

She propped her bare feet up on the dash. "I guess. I just assumed no one wanted to date you."

Cash's jaw came unhinged as he glanced at the girl. No humor showed on her face. "Are you joking?"

"Kind of." Her lips quirked up for a moment. "But you are my brother. That's weird."

He kept his focus on the white lines in front of him. "What would you think if I did date someone?"

"You mean Coach Grayson?"

Cash nodded.

"Why would I care? I like her better than you anyway."

Aunt Libby was right on one count. "You are on fire today."

Now his sister sported a full-fledged smile. "If anything, I've been wondering what's wrong with you. I thought maybe you didn't have the nerve to ask her out."

He'd just ignore that jab. "But I thought…Olivia

said that when the two of you went to Austin to go dress shopping, you overheard Aunt Libby talking to her about me and that you looked upset. We thought you were upset about us. And then when you got back from that trip, you were so crabby." He swung an apologetic look in her direction. "You seemed unhappy."

Rachel sighed. "I was upset after that trip."

He knew it.

"But I wasn't upset about the two of you." Rachel crossed her arms and glanced out her window. "I was upset because I kept getting texts from people who'd seen Blake out with some other girl."

Despite the good news that she hadn't been upset with him, Cash's heart plummeted. "Was he cheating?"

She shrugged. "I don't know. He said he wasn't, but I couldn't decide if I believed him."

Cash flexed white knuckles around the steering wheel. And he hadn't liked the boy before...

"You don't have to freak out. Coach Grayson and I talked about Blake after the incident and I broke up with him."

Huh. So really, Cash should be sending Rachel to live with Olivia.

"So." When Cash continued, Rachel groaned. "I always thought that if I didn't date...that you'd get all of my attention and that maybe..."

"Maybe what?"

"That you'd have as great an upbringing as I had. That you'd feel loved and confident and—"

"And not screw up?" Rachel gave a cynical laugh. "How's that working for you, brother?" She continued before Cash could say anything, feet dropping to the floor mat as she turned slightly toward him. "Let me tell you this. Whether you date anyone or not—that is, if you can find someone who'd say yes—doesn't matter to me. If anything, you're better with Coach Grayson around. She kind of…mellows you out."

Huh. "So you wouldn't feel cheated?"

"No, all right already? I know you do everything for me, and now I find out you've given up everything for me? I don't want that kind of pressure. Would you?"

No. He wouldn't.

Rachel popped her earbuds in, signaling the end of the conversation, but it only felt like the beginning for Cash.

He might have figured out what Rachel thought about his dating, but now he needed to figure out what God thought. And that felt like a whole different battle.

Olivia entered the short-term parking lot at the Austin airport. Thursday-night traffic hadn't amounted to much, so she'd gotten there faster than planned. Now she had tomorrow off and the whole weekend with her sister.

Cash had been so busy that Olivia hadn't seen him in almost two weeks, except for a glimpse at church. Twelve days to be exact. And while she should feel relieved about having the time to figure out what to say to him and how to say it, the space only increased the humming tension she felt. After Lucy left, Olivia would track Cash down and follow through on her plan to tell him about Josh and her miscarriage.

For now, she'd relax into this weekend with her sister. Three nights of distraction, of not thinking about Cash or the mess she'd created. She'd been walking around saying a verse from Psalm 103: "As far as the east is from the west, so far has He removed our transgressions from us." If only it felt that way. She'd taped every verse on forgiveness she could find to her bathroom mirror. Lucy would probably think she'd gone crazy. Olivia would tape one on her forehead if it would just sink through her hard skull. Somehow, she and God were going to figure out this forgiveness thing together. Even if she broke again trying.

Olivia parked, going inside to meet Lucy instead of driving through passenger pickup like they'd talked about. Ten minutes later, she spotted her sister through the upstairs glass. Halfway down the escalator, Lucy started waving and squealing. She waited impatiently for the people on the escalator to clear into the baggage claim area, then flew at Olivia.

The enthusiastic hug almost knocked Olivia over, and they garnered plenty of attention with their dramatics. Olivia held on to her sister, surprised to find tears forming. She'd missed this crazy woman.

Lucy's ash-blond hair hung down her back in loose curls, and she stood a half foot shorter than Olivia. No one would recognize they were sisters except for the blue of their eyes. Even their fashion sense differed. While Olivia opted for simple—jeans, ballet flats and a striped shirt—Lucy looked like a fashionable gypsy. Inches of bangle bracelets lined one wrist, and her flowing bright orange shirt was accented with a beaded turquoise necklace. Skinny jeans and heeled brown ankle boots completed the look.

Lucy linked her arm with Olivia's, propelling her toward the guitar-themed baggage claim as live music floated down into the open space.

"Why didn't you just pack a carry-on?"

Her sister laughed. "You'll see in a minute." When the bright orange-and-pink striped bag came down the conveyor belt, it took two of them to lug the monstrosity off the carousel.

"Is this thing hand painted?"

Lucy beamed. "How else am I supposed to recognize it?"

"What did you pack? You're only going to be here three nights."

"I know you told me the weather would be nice, but you just never know. So I needed two outfits for every day, depending on whether it would be warm or cool. And all of that might have fit in a carry-on..." Lucy paused and Olivia imagined a drumroll. "Until I started on coordinating shoes."

Olivia chuckled, basking in the essence of Lucy. Her sister had been headstrong and adventurous even as a baby. Lucy followed the rules—she just tried to make the experience as fun as possible.

They walked toward short-term parking, Lucy pulling the suitcase that earned more than a few curious looks. After loading up, Olivia drove to Curra's Grill. They snagged a table on the patio and munched on chips and salsa while Lucy told Olivia stories from her last year of college.

"So, what's your plan when you're finished with school?" Olivia shifted back from the table when their food arrived. The server checked Lucy out, but she continued talking, oblivious to the young man's attention or the way his spiked hair and plentiful ear piercings seemed to perk up with interest. "I'm still trying to decide. I'd love to work at a dance school, but teaching a few classes won't pay the bills. I know I need to put my business degree to work, but—" Lucy shrugged. "I also don't want to sit behind a desk all day."

"I can't really see that happening."

"I know, right?" Lucy grinned.

"What about the dance place you're already teaching at part-time?"

She took a bite of her enchiladas. "I asked. They don't have any more hours for me, and they don't need any help in the office."

"I guess we'll have to pray about it."

No worry marred Lucy's smooth complexion. "Exactly. God can handle it."

Oh, to be young and innocent and *trusting* again. Olivia shook off the guilt before it could sink claws into her skin. Enough! She was working on it.

After they finished, the server cleared their plates and asked if they wanted dessert, his eyes never straying from Lucy. Maybe a few jumping jacks would gain the man's attention. Lucy ordered for them, and when he walked away, Olivia laughed. "Sis, you've got an admirer."

Lucy tucked a wedge of curls behind her ear and leaned forward. "I hadn't noticed. But I did notice you failed to bring up one topic of conversation."

Why had Olivia ever said anything to Lucy about Cash?

"Out with it. What's the latest with the cowboy? When do I get to meet him?"

"You don't."

"Why?" A line cut through Lucy's forehead.

"Because…I just don't have any plans for you to meet him."

Lucy waited while the server deposited their dessert on the table along with their check. After a generous spoonful of chocolate mocha cake, she turned her attention back to Olivia. "How am I going to decide what to call him if I don't even get to meet him?"

"You could call him Cash, since that is his name." Olivia took a bite, wishing this conversation would disappear as fast as the piece of cake between them. Not even chocolate made this better.

Lucy waved her spoon back and forth. "No way. *Way* too boring."

Olivia laughed.

"So really, tell me the latest."

What could she say? "Same old with us. We're not dating or anything, Lulu. We're just friends determined to help his little sister."

Lucy raised an eyebrow.

"I mean it. He's never even kissed me." But there had been a few moments that Olivia wondered if he might, and one almost kiss the night of the dance. Still, Olivia wasn't going to let her thoughts travel down that path. Nothing good could come from Cash breaking his promise to Rachel.

Lucy leaned forward. "Tell me this. Did you ever feel anything like this for Josh?"

Her sister only knew that Olivia and Josh had broken up, not the details of what had shattered her heart before and after that breakup. But Olivia sensed she couldn't as easily hide this truth from her sister—or herself.

She filled her lungs, letting the air out slowly. "No. Not even close."

"Liv, what are you going to do?"

Olivia didn't have an answer, so she tossed her sister's words back to her. "God can handle it."

Apparently her sister couldn't argue with that.

"This is crazy." The next evening, Olivia scanned her head-to-toe black clothing in the full-length mirror in her room. She had her hair pulled back into a ponytail and old tennis shoes on her feet. How had a Saturday evening girls' night turned into this?

"It's not that crazy. Besides, I look pretty good." Lucy rolled the top of her borrowed yoga pants over three times until they didn't drag on the ground. The long-sleeved black T-shirt she'd commandeered from Olivia's closet also dwarfed her frame, and Janie and Lucy dissolved into giggles. Again.

"You know, Janie, when I invited you to have dinner with us tonight, I thought you might be a *mature* influence in my sister's life."

Janie collapsed onto the bed. "I'm sorry." Her

smile betrayed her words. "I just thought, why not? I've lived here all of my life except for college and I've never done it."

"Because it doesn't make any sense." Olivia tried to keep her amusement from showing on her face. Someone needed to be the voice of reason in this room.

During dinner, Olivia and Janie had made the mistake of telling Lucy about the town tradition of posing for nighttime photos with the honorary school mascot. And Lucy's idea had been born.

"That's exactly why we should do it. We need to experience life, and this is one thing none of us have done. *Why not* is the real question."

Janie looked at Lucy with awe. "I'm guessing you probably never got into trouble."

"She didn't. She can finagle her way out of anything."

Lucy preened, looking hilarious in Olivia's clothes. How did her sister not have a black top and bottom in that overstuffed bag of hers? Hiking out to take pictures with a billy goat in the dark of night was not at all the way Olivia had expected to spend a Saturday evening with her sister. Although, really, why was she surprised?

And the unnecessary black clothes? Lucy's idea, of course.

Lucy put one arm over her head and leaned to the side.

"What are you doing?"

She switched arms and leaned in the other direction, giving Olivia a look that said her actions should be obvious. "I'm stretching."

Janie snickered, and despite her attempt not to, Olivia laughed. After Lucy did a few leg stretches, Janie popped up from the bed. "Let's go so I can get changed."

The three of them walked over to the Smiths' house. Janie went to change, and Olivia introduced her sister to Jack, who sat on the couch watching TV.

He twisted over the back of the couch to shake Lucy's hand, eyebrows raised. "You ladies committing some crime tonight?"

They shook their heads. According to Janie, the Colborns enjoyed their goat's legendary status and didn't mind teenagers traipsing out to their farm to take pictures with it.

Olivia wondered how they felt about teachers doing the same.

When Janie flew back into the room wearing black sweats and a black T-shirt, Jack chuckled and turned back to the TV, raising one hand over his head. "I don't want to know."

Janie looped her arms around Jack's neck from behind and kissed him on the cheek. "Love you, honey."

"Yeah, yeah. Love you, too."

They pushed the door open, Jack's voice following them into the night. "Don't call me when you get arrested. I'll be sleeping."

They giggled all the way to Janie's car.

Chapter Sixteen

Her students must have been making up stories, because Olivia didn't imagine the Colborns' goat had *ever* let anyone take a picture with it. Not only did they not have a photo with the three of them and the goat, Lucy had almost lost the tip of a finger.

Then, in their mad rush to get back to the car, the three of them had slipped and fallen in the mud from last night's rain. It had squished through Olivia's fingers and under her shoes like pudding. Though it smelled nothing like chocolate.

After doing her best to clean her hands with one of Tucker's wet wipes, Olivia brushed tears of laughter from her cheeks. *Thank You, God, for these two girls. What would I do without them?*

They parked on the street by Janie's house and walked to Olivia's apartment, mud dropping off them with each step. Olivia felt like a walking piece of plaster—the more the mud dried, the harder it became to move. She considered borrowing Mrs. Faust's garden hose to spray them off outside.

Lucy stopped at the bottom of the stairs and Olivia and Janie crashed into her.

"Why are you stopping?"

Her sister stepped to the side and Olivia found herself face-to-face with Cash, sitting two steps from the bottom.

The man's amused grin made Olivia want to crawl up the stairs and into her apartment.

Olivia made introductions, and Lucy's smile grew to one of victory. How did her little sister always get what she wanted?

Lucy faced Cash. "It's a pleasure to meet you, rancher-cowboy-man. Now, if you'll excuse me, I feel I may be in need of a shower."

Cash laughed and moved down the stairs so that Lucy could go up, but his eyes never left Olivia. Warmth echoed through her despite the cooling temperatures.

"McCowboy!" Lucy paused with one hand on the apartment doorknob, throwing a victory fist in the air. "I knew I'd think of something."

When she walked inside and Cash turned to Olivia for answers, she just raised her hands. "Don't even ask."

Janie cleared her throat behind Olivia. "I'm sure

Jack is wondering where I am." She took off down the driveway, leaving a muddy trail behind her.

"Do you have a second? I wanted to talk to you about something. Although—" Cash grinned "—maybe this isn't the best time."

Her heart thudded against her ribs. She needed to talk to him, too. "Sure." Olivia dropped down to the step, causing a cloud of dust to radiate from her clothes, and Cash sat next to her. Not only did he look amazing in a charcoal button-down shirt, jeans and boots, he smelled so good she wanted to lean closer and breathe him in. He didn't have a hat on tonight, leaving his golden-green eyes visible. They seemed so serious. What was going on? Was he sending Rachel to Austin?

"Lucy's in the shower or I'd go..."

Cash removed a piece of mud from behind her ear, causing Olivia's skin to prickle. "From what you've told me about your sister, this situation somehow makes sense. And you don't need to shower." He took in every inch of her face. "You're cute even covered in mud."

What? Cash normally did not make that kind of comment. He was always so...careful. And Olivia felt thankful for that. She needed that barrier between them, especially now, when she planned to be honest with him. How much harder would that be if they were more than friends?

"And...manure?"

At Cash's question, she glanced at her formerly blue, now mud-bathed tennis shoes, torn between embarrassment and laughter. "There might be a bit of that involved."

Cash laughed. "Now we're even, since you've seen me the same way."

Olivia pulled her ponytail to the shoulder away from Cash, giving him full access to her profile and neck. Even smelling like the ranch and dusted in mud, she made his pulse take off at a sprint.

"So, what's up?"

Over the last two weeks, Cash had been meeting with Pastor Rick. He'd realized a number of things during their counseling sessions, and each time he learned something new, he wanted to share it with one person...Olivia. But between the ranch and the meetings, Cash had barely fit in time for meals. Every day he got up before the sun and went to bed long after it set.

"I had something good happen with Rachel."

Olivia glanced up with interest from the muddy fingernails she'd been scraping. The fact that the woman next to him obviously loved his sister only made her more attractive. More irresistible.

"Are you going to tell me what you girls were doing, by the way?"

"Maybe later." She smiled. "Tell me what happened with Rachel."

Cash told her about the trip to Austin and the conversation on the car ride home. "So Libby and Dean don't feel like she should move to Austin, and she wasn't upset about us."

"I'm so glad to hear we didn't make things worse. I assume that means Rachel's staying?"

"Yep."

At his answer, her lips tipped up with pure joy. "That is really good news."

He couldn't help memorizing her face. It felt like months since he'd seen her. "I've missed you."

By the way Olivia's mouth formed an O, Cash imagined she hadn't been expecting that kind of statement from him. He'd never allowed himself to say it before, but now, after talking to Pastor Rick, he felt the freedom. It felt good. Except for the way Olivia's nose scrunched up and she studied the stairs under them instead of him. That part didn't feel very hopeful.

Was she embarrassed? Or just trying to help him keep his promise about Rachel? He was about to find out.

"After I realized that my promise wasn't helping Rachel, I needed to figure out if I'd made the whole thing up or if God wanted me to make a promise like that."

He had Olivia's attention now. "What did you figure out?"

"I met with Pastor Rick. I didn't want to throw

away years of commitment because—" *Because I wanted you.* "Anyway, we prayed about it, and then I decided to fast about it, too. God brought me to a number of verses about control, and I finally accepted that I did come up with it on my own." Cash couldn't believe how much lighter he felt since then.

He stretched his legs out in front of him. "I thought that if I controlled everything with Rachel, if I tried hard enough, if I gave her every ounce of my attention, that she would have a better life. Pastor Rick challenged me to give that control back to God instead of trusting in myself and my ability to parent. I'm not saying it's going to be easy, but I'm trying."

Olivia's eyes widened, and she took a deep breath. "That…is really great news." Her hand brushed across his shoulders. "I think this back could use a break from all of that stress. I'm so glad to hear you're not going to attempt everything on your own anymore."

"Me, too."

Concern etched into Olivia's forehead, but it quickly turned to excitement as she shifted toward him. "If you worked through that, did you…talk about anything else? Did you talk to Pastor Rick about your parents' deaths…or Tera?"

"No. We didn't talk about anything else. What about Tera?"

"Do you think…I mean—" Olivia's ponytail flew across her shoulders as her head shook back and forth. "I'll admit she's not my favorite person, and I'm no expert on forgiveness, but do you think you'll ever move past what happened?"

"I forgave Tera a while ago." His shoulders slipped up. "But there's a difference between forgiving and forgetting. She taught me a lesson that day. Lying has consequences. Nothing will change the fact that Tera's lie was my mom's death sentence. She'd already lied to me once by cheating, and I should never have trusted her again. Now, once my trust is broken, I'm done. Life's much simpler that way."

Olivia's hand pressed against her neck and she shifted forward again.

"Even with Rach…" Cash shook his head. "I'm still struggling over the lie she told me about that party. I don't know if I'll ever trust her again the way I used to. But she is my sister." He rubbed hands down his jeans and gave a short laugh. "So I guess I'm stuck with her even if I can't trust her."

Olivia looked a little green in the face. Had she encountered something tonight that would make her faint? Just what had the girls been doing?

She popped up from the step, and he resisted tugging her back down. Now what? Cash wanted to say something about them, but he couldn't find the words. After all of this time, he had the freedom, just not the guts like Rachel had said.

"Lucy's probably out of the shower by now. So I guess I better…" Olivia tilted her head toward the apartment. "But I'm glad to hear your good news."

Cash's heart dropped under the stairs. Was he really going to let her walk away? He stood and watched her jog up the stairs.

"Liv, wait." He followed, catching her at the top of the landing. "What are you doing for Thanksgiving? Can you come to the ranch? Libby and Dean will be there." *And me.*

She nibbled on her lower lip, and Cash fisted his hands to keep from hauling her into his arms.

"Sure. Thanks."

She walked into the apartment, and it took Cash minutes to make his feet work. He was walking away from the woman he wanted. Again. And this time he didn't even have an excuse.

Olivia towel dried her freshly showered hair and walked into the living room, expecting to find her sister sprawled out on the couch. Instead, she found Lucy in the bedroom spread across the double bed at a diagonal angle, sleeping soundly. Olivia tiptoed back out into the living room, knowing she wouldn't be able to sleep right now. Her body felt jittery. Unsettled. She wished she didn't know why.

Hearing Cash's news tonight had rocked her delicately balanced world. With Cash not believing in his promise not to date anymore, Olivia had feared he might say something about them…and then what would she say?

Over the last two weeks, Olivia had felt as though she was moving forward with letting go, with forgiveness. She'd expected to see Cash and tell him everything. Faith that Cash would be understanding, that God would meet her in that moment and give her strength had even begun to grow. But she hadn't imagined this kind of news. It changed everything. Because with the chance for something more between her and Cash, she had even more to lose.

For a moment tonight, she'd been so excited thinking maybe he'd processed his trust issues with Pastor Rick, hoping it would pave the way for what she needed to tell him.

But no. The lie she'd woven between them still haunted her, and after hearing what Cash had said about trust, how could she ever tell him now?

Thankfully he'd left tonight without saying more.

Olivia tossed her towel onto the back of the cream slipcovered couch, then went into the kitchen and made a package of ramen noodles in the microwave. She toyed with the sleeves of her white cotton T-shirt while she waited for the beep, nervous energy thrumming through her. After grabbing a spoon, she took the bowl from the microwave and sat on the couch, tucking her legs beneath her. She wore her third and last clean pair of yoga pants. Good thing she had enough—not that she'd ever done yoga—to keep herself and her sister supplied.

She turned on *You've Got Mail*, but it didn't have the typical calming effect. Olivia finished the ramen and set the empty bowl on the coffee table. After a bit, she shifted to a reclining position, but instead of watching the movie, she studied the ceiling. She jumped up and went back to the kitchen, searching the cupboard next to the refrigerator. Finding a package of Dove Promises, she took two, then changed her mind and grabbed a third. Traipsing through a pasture definitely earned her an extra chocolate.

Olivia unwrapped the blue foil and popped one in her mouth, almost choking when she read the promise on the inside.

Hold on to love.

What kind of promise was that? She balled the wrapper and threw it in the trash can, then unwrapped the second. Not going to read that one. They were like strange chocolate fortune cookies that made no sense. She bought them for the chocolate but for some reason could never resist checking the message.

Not tonight.

After finishing the third, she threw the other

wrappers in the trash, surprised when her phone beeped. At this time of night it would normally be Lucy. But since her sister was asleep in the other room… Olivia grabbed her phone off the kitchen table and checked the text.

It was from Cash.

Are you up?

A wry smile curved her lips as she texted back.

Yes.

What had Rachel done now? Olivia almost dreaded the next text.

Open your door.

Olivia dropped the phone onto the table with a clatter. Had he left a note? A package? She yanked open the door, startled to see him there. "Cash? What's wrong?"

He grabbed her hand and tugged her onto the landing, pulling the door shut behind her.

"Is Lucy up?"

She'd barely shaken her head when Cash's hands stilled the movement, his lips descending on hers with a need and desire she understood well.

Oh, my. How long had she wanted this with this

man? Pretty much since she'd laid eyes on him in her classroom. But then she hadn't had all of the friendship and history pulling her in, making him irresistible. Olivia let herself fall into the kiss, into the softness of his lips and the way his warm hand slid under her still damp hair, urging her closer.

Cash gentled the kiss, but he didn't stop. Olivia didn't want him to stop. Ever. If she was only going to kiss the man once, she might as well enjoy every moment.

His lips left hers to press soft kisses against her closed eyelids. "Liv." The warmth of her name whispered along the corners of her mouth. "You taste like chocolate."

He lowered his forehead to hers, and Olivia left her eyes closed. Maybe if she didn't look, the moment would never end.

"Hey." Cash's hoarse voice broadcast a smile. "I have a question to ask you."

Olivia opened her eyes, seeing all the words he hadn't said written across his face.

"Will you go on a date with me?"

She wanted to say yes so badly. She wanted to pull him back down until his lips met hers again, ignore the tears fighting for release, and pretend she hadn't lied, that her painful past didn't stand between them like a bodyguard.

Her fingers skimmed up his arms, his warm skin begging her to tug him closer, to let him make all of her mistakes disappear, if only for a minute. His mint breath hovered over her lips, and she held back a groan at him being so close, offering her everything she wanted but couldn't have.

"I—I can't."

Cash's fingers froze at the back of her neck, his Adam's apple bobbing.

"I need some time. I need to pray about…some things."

His hand fell like a rock, taking her heart with it. Cash tried to wipe the hurt from his face, but Olivia knew it would stay in her mind like a photo she couldn't delete. A fitting reminder of the pain she'd caused.

As Cash drove away, Olivia finally knew the answer to the question she'd asked herself after the volleyball tournament. Was she in love with Cash Maddox?

Yes. So much that her heart ached at the knowledge, and her breath stuttered with panic at the thought that she'd just let him walk away without telling him everything.

She leaned back against her apartment door, sliding down until she crashed on the landing. She wanted Cash forever, wanted to handle everything life threw their way—including Rachel—together.

It should be the best news, realizing she loved Cash, but instead it felt like a crushing blow.

Because the only way to keep him—telling him the truth—was the one thing that guaranteed she would lose him.

Chapter Seventeen

W̲hat was wrong with him?

Cash threw the bag of dog food for Cocoa into the back of the truck along with the rest of the supplies he'd picked up, then slammed the tailgate shut. He strode to the driver's side door and hopped in, feeling a bit like Rachel when he almost took the door off the hinges.

When a woman said she needed to pray about something, a man said "Yes, ma'am," walked away and let her. But with each passing day that he didn't know what held Olivia back, Cash's impatience grew. She'd come to Thanksgiving at the ranch, and they acted like friends, but they rarely saw each other outside of Olivia tutoring Rachel.

The worst part? Cash missed his best friend. And he didn't know how to get her back. Had he been wrong all this time? Had he imagined her having feelings beyond friendship for him? He hadn't imagined that kiss. There had to be some truth in that moment.

He groaned thinking about it—about how he'd like a repeat performance. If only his brooding would quit when he turned in to the ranch drive, but if the last few weeks were any indication, it had built a house right next to his and planned to stay.

He didn't like this side of himself. Olivia had been his biggest support with Rachel and his commitment not to date. He should do the same for her, but his patience seemed to be running out. Especially now that he had the freedom to ask her for a relationship. Yet that option had been tabled, and Cash didn't know how much longer he could go without asking what held her back.

He needed to talk to her. Tonight at the championship football game in San Antonio, he'd track her down. Surely she could share with him what worried her—and most importantly, what held her heart. That question concerned him the most, because he'd thought the answer would be him. Cash would never push her into a relationship, but he had to ask. Maybe he could pray about it, too. They were friends, and every time he did see her, she seemed sad. And that might be his least favorite thing about this whole situation.

The Alamodome filled with cheers as the Billies ran off the field at halftime. Janie had left Tucker at home with her parents so she could enjoy the game, but she seemed too filled with energy and nerves to actually sit still. In the first half, she'd popped out of her seat more times than Olivia could count.

"Relax. Jack can handle it and we're seven points ahead." Olivia tugged on her friend's hand, but Janie didn't sit even as the people in the stands around them filtered out to get snacks during the break. "Besides, it's just a football game."

That got her attention. Janie swung in Olivia's direction. "You definitely can't call yourself a Texan with that kind of attitude."

"I'm joking. I'm just as nervous for Jack as you are." *Maybe not quite.*

Janie wrung her hands. "I'm going to pop down by the locker room and see if I can catch him on the way back out."

Olivia watched her friend scoot down the row and then stood herself, stretching arms over her head. She needed a break from sitting, and she could use a soda. Scanning the crowd behind her, she relaxed after finding no sign of Cash. She knew he was here, but she didn't know what to say to him. Olivia had been on her knees since their kiss, praying for some answers, some way out of this mess she'd made. If God forgave her for the past, why couldn't she move on? Why couldn't she tell Cash the truth?

She still didn't know the answer to that first

question. But the second answer came easily. The fear that Cash wouldn't forgive her for lying kept her paralyzed.

At the top of the stairs, Olivia made her way to the concessions line. After a wait, she purchased a Diet Coke. When she turned from the counter, the face she saw made her stomach jump with a mixture of dread and excitement. Cash stood across the crowd, wearing the same vintage gray Billies T-shirt he'd worn the night they'd first talked about his promise not to date—the night she'd kept her past from him without realizing what she'd done.

He slowly made his way through the people until he stood in front of her, nudging one of her red-and-white Asics with his gray tennis shoe.

"New shoes?" He raised an eyebrow with the question.

"Had to replace the pair ruined by the goat."

Since she'd told them the story at Thanksgiving, Cash laughed.

Olivia had also hoped that a new pair of tennis shoes would lift her spirits in the way jewelry or flowers did for most girls. It hadn't worked.

His eyes traveled up her jeans and red Billies hoodie, landing on her face with a smile. Despite the stress of seeing him, her lips tipped up in response to his. No denying it. She'd missed this man. She'd fallen head-over-flip-flops in love with him, and he didn't have a clue because she didn't know how to tell him that or anything else she needed to tell him.

He tilted his head. "You want to walk around a bit during halftime?"

A walk in a public place couldn't make anything worse than Olivia already had. She accepted and they moved forward.

"Rachel's talking about going to Colorado for college."

Olivia glanced at Cash, but the typical worry didn't cover his face.

"To my dad?"

"Yep."

Olivia felt a real smile for the first time in weeks. "That's great news. My dad would be so good for her. He's such a great coach. Not that I'm biased."

Cash nudged her shoulder with his. "I'm a little biased myself toward his daughter."

You shouldn't be. They greeted a few parents from school before the crowd thinned as people returned to their seats. Olivia turned her attention back to Cash as they continued walking. "How do you feel about Rachel going out of state?"

"I'm all about letting go."

"Really?"

Cash laughed. "Nope. But I'm working on it."

At least the man was honest. Unlike her.

"So listen, I was hoping we could talk. I know you need time, and I want to give you that, but I'm also—" Cash stopped walking and Olivia paused with him. "I'm struggling with patience. I know you were patient with me, and I want to be the same for you."

Who knew she could hurt in so many places at once?

"Anyway, if it's something you can tell me, then maybe I can pray about it too."

Olivia's heart sank to the floor. How could she tell him here? In the middle of a football game? But she did need to talk to him. Even if she lost him in the process, it would be better than this. "We should talk." The words almost choked her. "After the game?"

"Sure. Ride back with me?"

The hour drive back to Fredericksburg would be the perfect opportunity for Olivia to bare her soul, tell Cash the truth...and possibly lose him forever. "That works."

Cash glanced around the now-empty concessions area before taking one step toward her, then another. Olivia retreated until her back hit the wall, air whooshing out of her.

He stood close enough that with a slight lean, his lips could touch hers. One arm snaked around her to press against the wall, and his other hand came up, thumb slipping across the traitorous area that now held back a whimper.

"You know what, Liv Grayson? You are hard

not to kiss." He paused. Swallowed. Pushed off the wall and took a step back. "But I'll wait until you're ready. You're worth waiting for."

Those words… *You're worth waiting for.* Hope burst from a dormant ember to a roaring fire inside of her. Maybe they had a chance. Didn't she know his heart? She had to believe he'd meet her confession with grace.

Olivia fisted her hands in the front of his T-shirt, tugging him forward until they were only a moment apart. She rose slightly until her lips were parallel with his and drowned herself in his eyes, wishing she could say the words out loud.

Love me. Don't give up on me.

And then, because her heart felt too achingly full to say all of that, because she might only have today, she whispered two little words.

"Kiss me."

Cash pulled her behind a wall that blocked them from any remaining parents or students, and then he did exactly that.

Pandemonium erupted as the kick went through the goalposts, pulling the Billies further ahead and clinching the win. State champions. Cash cheered and whistled, laughing as the team doused Jack with ice. He'd have liked to get in on that part.

Jack looked up into the stands until he found Janie and waved. She looked like a blubbering mess from Cash's vantage point twenty rows up. She kept alternating between cheering, crying, and hugging Olivia. Cash would have liked to get in on that last part, too. And hopefully he would. Maybe tonight, if that kiss was any indication. He felt so giddy that he got Olivia to himself for the ride home that if Jack knew his thoughts right now, his friend would never stop making fun of him. *Ever.*

Cash went down onto the field with the rest of the crowd and spent about an hour celebrating, congratulating Jack and the rest of the players. It brought Cash right back to high school. They'd gone to state, but they hadn't won. Now Jack had the championship ring he deserved for so many years of hard work.

Rachel waved from where she stood with a group of her friends—including Blake Renner. Concern rolled through Cash's gut. The fact that Renner had come to support the team even though he wasn't eligible to play showed some maturity. But it didn't stop Cash from giving thanks that Blake stood across the circle from Rachel instead of next to her.

His goodwill had limits.

He spotted Olivia and made his way through the throng of people in her direction. "You ready?"

Olivia held his gaze for a long minute before nodding. "I am." A light filled her eyes that hadn't been there in a while. She hugged Janie and said goodbye.

"Actually—" she grinned at him "—I need to use the restroom and then I'm ready to go."

They walked up the stairs and Cash reached for her hand. Her fingers threaded through his, and when she glanced up with those big blue eyes, his heart tumbled.

This woman definitely turned him into the biggest sap on the planet.

Olivia grabbed her purse from the back of the bathroom door and slipped it on her shoulder, taking a deep breath that didn't do anything to calm her. Her hands had a slight tremor, but despite the trepidation holding her captive, she knew what she had to do. Olivia didn't want to live with the past or this lie holding her down anymore.

Tonight, she would tell Cash. And she prayed that somehow he would meet her with grace and forgiveness.

She started to turn the lock, pausing when a voice from outside the stall made her wince.

Tera. Ugh.

Olivia jerked her hand back. It wasn't that Olivia couldn't handle the woman. Just that right now, she didn't want to deal with anything but the conversation she needed to have with Cash.

"Hey, sweetie. How are you? How are things with that boyfriend of yours?"

Great. Tera had started a new conversation. If Olivia left the stall now, she'd hardly be able to escape. It would look as if she'd been eavesdropping. Which she was doing, but not on purpose.

Olivia got the hand sanitizer from her purse and squirted it on her palm.

"How did you know? We actually just got back together."

The voice that answered Tera made Olivia's world spin to a stop. She would recognize Rachel's voice anywhere. And that comment...Olivia must have misheard. Rachel had gotten back together with Blake? When? Why? She hadn't said a thing to Olivia about it. Every time the girl took two steps forward she seemed to take one giant leap back. That boy was not good news. And Cash would not be happy about this.

"That's so great!" Tera bubbled, and Olivia barely resisted running out of the stall and muzzling her. "You're being safe, right?"

Olivia reeled back. Tera *had not* just said that. Rachel would never—

"I think..." Rachel's voice lowered, and Olivia strained to hear. "I think we might, you know, for the first time."

Gripping her purse strap between white knuckles, Olivia resisted the urge to turn around and be sick.

"I know you kids are going to do what you're going to do, so I always tell my girls to be safe."

Safe. Olivia wanted to scream. There wasn't one thing safe about it. How could Tera go around spreading lies and influencing girls like this?

Their voices stopped, and after waiting a few seconds to make sure she no longer heard them, Olivia scrambled from the stall. She only spared the sink a glance, knowing she couldn't risk even one moment of not finding Rachel. Especially if this *event* were to happen tonight.

In the hallway, Cash stood from where he'd been leaning against the wall waiting for her.

"Have you seen your sister?"

He pointed to the left. "She went that way."

"I have to talk to her. I'm sorry. I'll be back."

Olivia took off at a jog and spotted Rachel just ahead. "Rach, wait up."

Rachel did, and Olivia caught up to her before she had time to process what she was going to say. She tugged the girl around the corner to the stairs entrance leading into the stadium. Not exactly private, but hardly any people still milled about this late after the game.

Now what?

"Rachel." Olivia swallowed a few times and tried to still her shaking hands. Her voice dropped to a whisper. "Were you just in the bathroom talking about Blake?"

Rachel's eyes flew wide open, and a hand covered her mouth. She shook her head, then stopped. "Yes. Are you going to yell at me?"

"No." Emotions tightened her throat. "Oh, Rachel. Why?"

She crossed her arms and shrugged. "He loves me. We talked about the past few months and he apologized. Before this we'd been dating for a year and I've been making him wait all this time. I just—I love him, and he says that if I love him and trust him, that…"

She didn't have to finish the words. "That's not love, Rach. Asking you for something like that isn't love."

Rachel's eyes narrowed. "What if I don't want to wait? What if I don't think it matters anymore?"

Olivia struggled for air, feeling as though someone held her head underwater. She had a choice. She could tell Rachel about her own past and hope it helped…or she could keep it to herself.

If it could help at all, if it could save Rachel from making the same mistake…Olivia had to tell her. She shifted, then held back a gasp at what she saw in her peripheral vision. Cash had followed her. Since Rachel stood tucked behind the wall at the entrance to the stairs, she couldn't see him. But from her position at the corner…Olivia could.

He stood a few yards away behind a closed concessions cart. By his shuttered eyes and the way he looked as if he'd been kicked by a horse, Olivia knew he'd heard the first half of her conversation with Rachel. Which meant if she told Rachel everything, Cash would hear at the same time.

The tears Olivia had been fighting all day begged for release. Before, she'd held out hope that if she confessed her lie to Cash, if she told him everything, that maybe, just maybe, he'd be able to forgive her for not telling the truth.

But now? If he heard her tell Rachel?

He'd never forgive her.

She could wait and tell him, but Olivia couldn't let Rachel suffer like that. Not when she knew the pain that would come from Rachel making the decision she planned to make.

Olivia took a small step forward so that the wall blocked the visual of Cash from her mind, but it didn't erase the truth that he still stood, listening to every word she said.

"There was another teacher at my old school in Denver. At first I didn't plan to be more than friends with him because we didn't share the same beliefs, but with persistence, he wore me down. Eventually, we started dating. I had always wanted to wait until marriage, but with time, that felt less and less important."

Rachel crossed her arms, but she nodded.

"I was tired of waiting for some perfect man that didn't exist. I walked away from God, from His plan, thinking I knew better." Olivia wiped her cheeks. "I didn't think it mattered anymore."

Teenage voices sounded behind her, and Olivia waited for them to pass by before continuing.

"I thought I was being smart. Safe." The word came out as a hiss. "But that stuff doesn't work all the time. And it does nothing to protect the rest of you."

This time, she had Rachel's full attention. The girl's arms fell to her sides. "What happened?"

"I got pregnant. When I told him, that's when I found out his true nature. He said he wasn't in the market for a family. He walked away as if I meant nothing to him. It was beyond awful. I was so stressed out, full of regret. Two weeks later, I miscarried."

Rachel's eyes widened, filled with a sheen of moisture, and her hand slipped up to cover her mouth.

"Losing the baby just added to my shame. I wondered if my stress caused the miscarriage. And…" Olivia's voice shook along with her body. "I still had to work at the same school with him. While I was suffering from the decisions I'd made and trying to function after the miscarriage, he moved on and started dating another teacher at our school. So all last year I had to deal with that." She shuddered and dug a tissue from her purse. "Every moment I want to go back. Every moment I wish someone would have pulled me aside and told me that something that seemed like nothing would become everything. That's the world's lie, Rachel Maddox. It matters."

It matters. Olivia stumbled under the weight of that truth. That's why she'd had such a hard time letting go of her past. It mattered, whether she was twenty-five or seventeen.

"God cares about you. Everything you do matters. And this—this is big. Way bigger than you know right now." Olivia grabbed Rachel's arms. "Don't do it. Don't make the same mistake I did. So many people love you. Cash loves you. Your aunt and uncle love you. I love you."

Tears streamed down Rachel's cheeks, and Olivia pulled the girl into a hug, thankful when she accepted the gesture. Rachel sniffled. "Thank you for telling me." That whisper held a lot of pain. Olivia imagined this one conversation wouldn't be enough, but they would have more. She'd make sure of it.

Rachel moved back, wiping under her eyes and coming away with black mascara. An eye roll followed. "I must look horrible."

Olivia smiled, thinking this felt like home territory with Rachel. "A little like that raccoon we saw."

That earned a grin from the teenager in front of her. Olivia wiped her own tears with the tips of her fingers. "I'm sure I'm no better. Thanks a lot for making me cry in a public place."

Rachel laughed. "I need to go find Val. I think I'm going to stay there tonight." Olivia had done everything she could. Now she would pray, pray, pray. "I promise I'll really go to Val's." Rachel stared at her hands. "I won't see Blake tonight."

Olivia's shoulders sagged in relief. "I'm here if you need anything."

"Thanks. And I won't tell anyone what you told me. I'm not that way."

"I know. I trust you." *And the one person I care about just found out in the worst possible way.*

Chapter Eighteen

Cash sank behind the closed concessions cart as his sister took off in the opposite direction.

The conversation he'd just heard made him want to keep sliding down until he hit the floor and then curl up in the fetal position. His baby sister. How could she even be thinking such a thing? Hadn't he talked to her so many times? Didn't his prayers work at all?

At least he could be thankful Olivia had talked to Rachel. His sister would never have listened to him like that. But then, he didn't have a story to tell that would have an impact the way Olivia's did. One Cash had never heard before. At first, he hadn't believed it was true, but then, as the details went on...

He buried his head in his hands. How could Olivia have kept something like that from him? What else hadn't she told him? Did he even know her at all? It wasn't that he didn't have grace over her past. If anything, the guy sounded like a jerk. But even when she knew how much he craved the truth, even when she knew how much it mattered to him, she had lied.

"Cash?"

He looked up. Olivia stood in front of him, looking as tormented as he felt. Must have been hard on her, actually telling the truth.

"I'm so sorry." Her hands twisted, then slipped into the pockets of her red sweatshirt. "I didn't want you to find out like that."

He stood and crossed his arms, fingers digging into his biceps until the knuckles went white and the skin underneath turned red. "How did you want me to find out? Were you ever planning to tell me?"

Her mouth opened and shut. Moisture filled her eyes and spilled down her cheeks, but she didn't wipe it away. "You—" Her voice wobbled along with her head. "You wouldn't believe me if I told you."

The sight of this woman in tears… While she'd taken his heart and trampled it, he could barely tamp down the urge that begged him to sweep across the space and comfort *her*.

He felt beaten. Betrayed. That last word was the one he needed to remember. Because he knew better than to let someone betray him twice.

"I asked you at the hospital and you said you were only upset about Janie. All of this time and you never said a thing. You even implied... We talked about what we wanted that night after the football game." Disbelief filled his lungs with cement. "You never gave any indication. Not once."

Olivia's whimper bounced off him as a deep breath shuddered from his chest. "I thought you were nothing like Tera, but I guess that's not true." Something cold took over his body, his words. "No wonder you were so curious what I thought about her. Neither of you seem to realize lying affects the lives of those around you. Neither of you cares about anything but yourselves."

That spark of *something* flashed in Olivia's eyes. She took a step forward, and he half expected a finger to poke into his chest. "I am *nothing* like Tera."

An hour ago he would have believed that, but right now he could barely think past the pain throbbing in his head. "Looks the same from where I'm standing."

Olivia took a step back from Cash and his hurtful words, feeling as though she'd been pummeled. Yes, she'd kept her past from him. She'd lied. She regretted it with everything in her. If she could go back—story of her life—she'd tell him earlier, before she'd ever let the lie pass through her lips, and erase the last few minutes of pain for both of them. But she couldn't. And nothing she said right now would make any difference. She could have said she'd planned to tell him tonight, but he would never believe her now.

Olivia had known this conversation wouldn't go well. She'd thought Cash would be hurt, wounded, but she hadn't expected him to lash out like this. And comparing her to Tera, saying she didn't care about anyone but herself…he obviously didn't know her at all.

All of this time she hadn't wanted her past to define her. Olivia had wanted to find a way to move forward and forgive herself. But now, she was right back where she'd started.

Would she never be more than the sum of her mistakes?

She took a step back, knowing she needed to escape. Again. "I'll find my own ride home." Hopefully Janie hadn't left yet. And Olivia still needed to track down the lovely Tera Lawton and have a few words with the woman.

When Cash didn't protest, didn't ask her to stay and work things out, didn't take back his pain-inducing words, Olivia turned and walked away. She thought she'd understood a broken heart before, but it didn't compare to this. Last time, she'd been broken into a thousand pieces. But now? More like a million.

So much for that new beginning.

* * *

"If you could redo one thing, what would it be?" Olivia closed the devotional after reading the last question. The morning light shone across Olivia's apartment table, her coffee and Rachel's Coke between them. "I guess you already know my answer to that question."

Rachel glanced to the side. "Yeah."

"What about you?"

Olivia had learned a few things about the girl in front of her over their last few meetings. She would talk about serious things, but she took her time.

So while Rachel studied her fingernails, Olivia waited. Since that night at the football game, she'd seen Rachel a number of times and they'd continued to talk about her future decisions. So far, Rachel had been very receptive, and Olivia prayed daily for a hedge of protection around the teenager.

But while Olivia had seen Rachel, she hadn't seen Cash.

He'd made himself scarce since the night of the football championship, and Olivia didn't blame him. She'd lied. She took full responsibility for that. And after the way Cash had responded, she didn't have any hope that they'd be able to work through this.

Somehow, she needed to adjust to the fact that their chance for something more was over…but it hurt. It felt a bit like her bones after the day she'd gone horseback riding with Cash. Only instead of healing, this pain stayed lodged right around her heart.

At least one good thing had come from that horrible night. Ever since she'd opened up to Rachel, Olivia had begun to feel the freedom she'd been longing for all of this time. She'd thought burying her past would liberate her from the guilt, but the opposite turned out to be true.

Too bad she'd figured that out too late.

"I guess—" Rachel's words pulled Olivia back to the present. "The day my parents died, I got into a fight with my mom right before they left." Rachel looked away, but when her gaze collided with Olivia's, the visible pain felt like a knife to her soul. "I wish our last words had been good."

Olivia wiped a few tears from her cheeks. She'd been so emotional lately, as if crying could purge the pain from her body.

"Do you think she hated me? Do you think she forgave me for being such a brat?"

For the love. Olivia needed a whole box of tissues for this conversation. How could Rachel have lived with that kind of hurt all of this time? Olivia prayed silently, wanting to choose her words wisely. "I may not have known your mom, but I know this. She loved you with a mother's love. It's like God's love. It's unstoppable. We can't do anything so bad that He won't love us anymore, and

I know your mom would have felt the same way. That's the beauty of grace."

We can't do anything so bad that He won't love us anymore.

Olivia's eyes momentarily fell shut. There it was. The reminder, the absolution she needed. The deliverance from her mistakes came too late for her and Cash, but hopefully not for Rachel.

"That's what I thought." Rachel tucked a lock of hair behind her ear. "But I just—it's good to hear it."

For me, too.

"You know, sometimes I think I learn more from this Bible study than you do."

Rachel laughed, and Olivia got up and retrieved the tissue box. Unlike herself, the teenager remained composed.

"I suppose you've got to get going." Rachel stood.

"I probably should." Though heading back to Colorado for Christmas didn't fill Olivia with the same joy it had only weeks ago. "Sorry I don't have much time."

"No problem. I'll see you when you get back?"

"Of course." Olivia hugged Rachel, then waved goodbye as the girl headed down the apartment stairs. She went back inside, grabbed her already packed suitcase and tugged it down the stairs.

After rolling over to Janie's, she knocked on the front door.

The inside door stood open, and when Tucker peeked through the glass storm door, Olivia left her suitcase on the step and let herself in. She scooped him up, kissing his sweet, baby powder-scented hair.

"Quit eating my son!" Janie came out of the kitchen smiling. "I'll be ready in a sec." She headed down the hall and Olivia tossed Tucker up in the air, ignoring the familiar longing in her chest when he giggled. She'd secretly begun to dream of this kind of life with Cash...but now she needed to move beyond that. Nothing would fill the chasm between them created by her lie and his response. How long would it take this hurt to ebb away? She couldn't fathom an answer that didn't discourage her.

When Janie reappeared, ready to go, the girls left Tucker with Jack, then headed for the Austin airport.

"Thanks for driving me all this way. You know that I could have left my car at the airport."

"It's not a problem. Besides, I think I might stay in Austin and shop for a bit." Janie glanced at Olivia with pink-tinged cheeks. "They have a certain store that I like and the doctor said it's okay to try again."

Despite the awfulness of the past weeks, joy

rushed through Olivia at seeing her friend filled with hope again. "Have you seen the way your husband looks at you? I don't think you need any of that."

Janie preened. "I am rather wonderful."

"And humble."

"Exactly." Janie's face went from amused to serious in seconds. "Any news with Cash?"

"No. He doesn't want to see me." She'd told Janie everything. Right down to the last detail. Again, she'd been greeted with grace. Tears. Hugs. Bless Janie, Olivia could have moved anywhere in the country, but God had definitely known she needed this woman in her life.

"You have got to talk to him. Apologize. Tell him why you lied. The two of you are the most stubborn people I've ever met. Both of you think you can control everything, neither of you—"

"He doesn't want to hear it!"

"Did you call him? Did you show up on his doorstep and camp out until he agreed to talk to you?"

Nope. Olivia hadn't done that and Janie knew it.

"This is what I'm talking about. You have to forgive yourself for the past *and* for lying to Cash. You had reasons. They might not have been perfect, but what's done is done. Time to forgive, girl."

"I have." *I think.* "I'm trying." And that was the truth. For the first time, Olivia felt the guilt over her past slipping away. She'd even begun to forgive Josh—though he'd probably never express remorse—choosing to praise God for rescuing her from that situation.

"Including Cash?"

Olivia crossed her arms.

"He didn't handle that moment well, but he was upset. Add him to your list of people to forgive. Maybe then you'd actually be able to go to him and talk to him about all of this."

Olivia wanted to be done with this conversation, but Janie's small car offered little escape. Probably calculated by the woman next to her.

"You're wearing some prideful britches to think that you know better than the God of the universe. His son already died for that forgiveness. For you and for that jerk ex-boyfriend of yours, for Cash, for me. It's done. The price has already been paid. Bless your heart, Liv, but you're like a homeless person who won't take handouts."

Goose bumps erupted across Olivia's skin. How did Janie pack that kind of punch with such sweetness?

"I think there's two kinds of guilt. The sinning kind, when God is telling you what you're doing isn't right, and then the kind where you dwell on mistakes so much that you're not worshipping God. One can be used for good. The other? You need to let go of."

Olivia sighed. "When did you get so smart?"

Janie winked. "I've always been brilliant."

Despite the serious subject, a laugh slipped out. Only Janie could throw all her words on the table in that manner and still come across as loving.

Janie joined in with her own laughter. "I'm sorry that all came flying out like that, but I had to say it. Trust me, I understand mourning for the baby you lost and the decisions you made." She sniffed. "That pain's not just going to go away. But the anger can. And forgiveness can change those wounds from bleeding and throbbing to an ache that heals over time."

As usual, Olivia imagined Janie wouldn't back down until she got what she wanted. But her friend didn't understand that Cash would never forgive Olivia. Since her plans didn't include talking to him, Olivia settled for a truth she could agree to. "I'll think about it."

"You think about it, and I'll do some praying." Janie's victory grin flashed. "That should soften that stubborn heart of yours a little quicker."

Chapter Nineteen

The ranch Jeep bumped in from the pasture, jarring Cash's stressed body. This morning he'd received a phone call from the grocery store in Austin that hadn't improved his already horrible mood. They'd partnered with another ranch, not him. Cash had been kicking around his disappointment ever since. Supplying the store wouldn't have been easy, but the extra income would have been nice. Especially with Rachel headed off to college at the end of summer. Still, it would have meant a larger herd, more ranch hands and even longer hours. Not that many more hours existed in a day.

Cash left the Jeep running by the garage, hopped out and opened the door, then drove inside. The ranch truck and Jeep needed an oil change, and Cash had volunteered. Frank and the other men had looked relieved. Between the store and what had happened with Olivia, Cash's mood had morphed from crabby to downright unbearable. No one wanted to be around him. When the ranch hands saw him coming, everyone scattered. Despite time to process, Cash still couldn't wrap his mind around the fact that Olivia had lied to him. He shouldn't be thinking about her at all, but his pigheaded brain didn't listen to logic anymore.

He pulled on the brake, turned off the ignition and jumped out just as his sister came in. "What's up?"

"Just came to find you."

Did the girl have good or bad news for him? Rachel hadn't been around much over Christmas break. Of course she spent Christmas at the ranch with Cash and Dean and Libby, but other than that, she'd been off traipsing with her friends most of the days. Cash could only pray and hope she wasn't doing what he'd overheard her talking to Olivia about. He'd confronted her the next day, and they'd talked, but short of locking her up, he didn't know how to protect her.

That probably wasn't helping his mood.

"So…how long are we going to have to deal with stompy, crabby Cash around here?"

He opened the hood. "As long as it takes."

"To do what? Get over Coach Grayson?"

Cash's hand stilled on the oil cap.

"Doesn't she come back tomorrow? What happened between you two anyway?"

Cash hadn't said anything to Rachel about what had happened between him and Olivia the night of the football game. Olivia must not have either if his sister still didn't know. Of course, it only took a little observation to decipher that he and Olivia hadn't seen each other since that night. He really did not want to discuss this with his little sister. Huh. That's probably what she felt like talking to him about boys.

"Did you want to discuss Blake again?" Cash finished removing the oil cap and winced at his own callousness.

Rachel crossed her arms. "I already told you I'm not going to do anything stupid. Unlike you, I've been talking to Coach Grayson. She's been helping me. You need to let this go. I'm working through it."

He tossed the cap onto the workbench with more force than necessary. He didn't like it when Rachel was right.

His sister slid backward onto the workbench, legs dangling in a carefree swing. "You should just give up everything you could have with Coach and hole up like you did after Mom and Dad died." Rachel's smooth voice brimmed with sarcastic sweetness she could patent. "Because your life was so much better when you lived that way."

Cash grabbed the socket wrench and oil pan, dropped to the ground, and slid under the Jeep.

"You should run and hide." She upped the volume of her voice. "Because you know what? People can hurt you." Her face appeared at the side of the Jeep where she bent down. "People disappoint. They make bad decisions. They drink with their friends, choose stupid boyfriends." Her voice whispered under the Jeep engine, ripe with pain and wobbling with emotion. "They can even die and leave you."

He sucked in a breath but continued working.

"So if you push away everyone you love, that would be safest." Rachel clapped her hands together slowly. "Bravo, brother. You managed to isolate yourself. No hurt there."

The oil gushed out into the pan as Rachel's words stabbed him.

Everyone you love.

Cash dropped an arm over his face.

He loved Olivia.

One mistake wouldn't change how he felt about her. Nothing could stop him from missing her, from needing her every second of the day.

"I don't get it anyway. Shouldn't you be upset with Ms. Lawton, not Coach?"

What? Cash pushed out from under the Jeep and faced his sister as she stood. "What did Tera do?"

Rachel's fingers landed on her throat. "Coach didn't tell you?" Her words were a strangled whisper.

Cash shook his head. When Rachel took a step back, he growled, "What happened?"

"She…" Rachel bit her lip.

"Rach, tell me."

She stalled, but eventually the story about what Tera had said in the bathroom spilled out of her. Cash balled his fists, tension radiating up his arms and into his shoulders. "Is that everything that happened?"

"Everything I was there for. But one of my friends said they saw Coach Grayson talking to Ms. Lawton that night as they were leaving the stadium. I guess it was a pretty big commotion. She said something to Ms. Lawton about never talking to me again. Told her to stay away from me or something like that." Rachel shrugged as though she didn't care, but her lips slid up. "Coach Grayson's tough. I like that about her."

He did too.

Rachel took a step back.

"Wait."

She paused, head tilted.

"I'm sorry I've been so ornery, and that I'm not better at helping you through the stuff with Blake." He grabbed a rag, wiping his grease-covered hands.

"I wish I could be more like Mom and Dad, that I could have given you the life you would have had with them." It didn't exactly fit the current conversation, but he needed to say it. He'd been thinking it for years. Cash took a steadying breath. "I'm sorry I'm not them. That I'm an idiot who doesn't know what I'm doing half the time."

"I never expected you to be Mom or Dad. And you're not an idiot." Her lips curved. "Those are words I never thought I would say." Amusement flashed across her face before she scowled and poked him on the chest. "You need to let go of feeling responsible for everything. You don't have to make up anything to me. Believe it or not, big brother, I think you've done a pretty good job." She slid the toe of her shoe across the dusty cement. "I mean, I know I'm not the easiest kid." Her green eyes met his, shimmering with just a hint of moisture. "But I thought we were doing okay."

Something unknotted in him. They were doing okay. They'd had a couple of close calls, but each time *someone* had protected his sister, and it hadn't been him.

"Besides, in a few more months I'll be off to college and out of your hair."

"Would you believe I'm not quite ready for you to be out of my hair?"

She smiled. "Maybe." Her arms crossed. "Don't

think the change in subject means you're off the hook about Coach."

The way she sounded like the older sibling made him tamp down a smile. But not one part of him had forgotten about Olivia.

"If there's anything I've learned in the last few weeks, it's that God's in charge of our lives. He sent Coach Grayson to fight for me." Her eyes narrowed. "He sent her for you, too. Now this is a case where you're treading awfully close to idiot. You'd better figure it out before you lose her altogether."

He definitely didn't like it when his sister was right.

"Are we good here?" Rachel waved a hand between them, eyebrow quirked. "Did we solve all of your issues?"

His mouth hitched. "Don't you have somewhere to be?"

She laughed. "Always." Her Converse shoes kicked up dust as she took off, giving a wave over her shoulder on her way out of the garage.

The knowledge that he couldn't make up their parents' deaths to Rachel—that she didn't expect him to—filled him with relief. But at the thought of Olivia, tension tightened his muscles again.

He'd assumed a lie made Olivia just like Tera. But that couldn't be further from the truth. He owed her an apology. And a thank-you. She must have confronted Tera *after* he'd been a jerk.

The way he'd responded to Olivia the night of the football championship came rushing back, ripping into his soul. She might have lied about her past, but when it came to protecting Rachel, she'd been willing to give up her secret. She would have known even while she told Rachel the story that he would be upset, yet she'd done it to save his sister.

He'd thought he'd worked through his control issues…but it turned out he still needed some work. Especially in the area of trust.

Cash had a choice to make. He could either cling to control and live life alone like Rachel said, or he could trust God instead of himself. Trust that God had placed Olivia in his life because she was exactly who he needed, exactly who Rachel needed. Trust that he did know her heart.

Olivia had most likely been too scared or wounded to tell him about her past when she had the opportunity. And now he'd only added to that pain. All because he couldn't trust, because he didn't want to get hurt again, just like his mouthy, wise little sister said.

Maybe when the snarky girl went off to college, she should get a counseling degree.

Olivia's return to Texas filled her with excitement and trepidation. Once again, she'd worked through her past, telling her parents and sister the truth about what happened with Josh. Each time she did, Olivia felt her freedom increase. She'd taken a walk through the Garden of the Gods by her parents' house and had a big conversation with God…and when she left that place, she knew she'd turned over another new leaf. She'd be fighting for forgiveness from now on. Every time guilt or shame tried to slip into her mind, she would send it right back out again.

Janie had been right…though Olivia hadn't relished telling her on the drive back from the airport. Her friend had also been happy to know that Olivia had a ranch field trip planned for this afternoon. She needed to talk to a certain cowboy and apologize for not telling him the truth. Though Cash's response had wounded her, Olivia knew his words had been spoken from a place of hurt…and that they weren't true. She planned to use this new superpower she had and *forgive* him. Even if Cash couldn't move past her lie, Olivia knew one thing: she would forgive herself this time. She wouldn't live her life like that anymore.

Olivia pulled up to the ranch house and stopped in front. She tore up the stairs before she lost her nerve and knocked on the front door. Colorado had been spitting cold when she left, but despite the much warmer Texas weather and the fact that Olivia wore jeans with her favorite waffle-knit blue cardigan sweater, she still shivered. She scuffed the sole of one brown ballet flat across the Maddox porch as she waited for someone to answer.

Rachel opened the door, greeting Olivia with a hug that went a long way toward calming her jumpy heart.

She followed the teenager inside. "Is your brother home?"

"No. He's out on the ranch somewhere."

Olivia didn't want to wait and give herself the opportunity to back out of her plan. She had to talk to him. Now. "Any chance I could borrow a Jeep? And you could point me in the right direction?"

Rachel rolled her eyes, but the smile that accompanied the look told Olivia her true feelings. A set of keys slid along the kitchen counter. "You can take mine."

Olivia grabbed them. "Thanks, Rach!" She rushed out the front door and over to Rachel's Wrangler, yanking open the driver's door. Stick shift. Why hadn't she ever learned how to drive one of these things?

"Give me the keys." Rachel stood behind her, palm out. "I'll give you a ride."

Olivia gave her the keys and a hug, eliciting a laugh.

"Coach, I didn't know you were such a sap."

She flew around the Jeep and into the passenger seat. "Only over your brother."

Rachel groaned, but as the Jeep dipped and

bumped over the rough terrain, the girl's lips curved again.

Finally, they spotted the old ranch truck. Rachel pulled up and Olivia hopped out. "Thanks!"

"You're welcome. Don't let him go all stubborn on you. He's got some issues. You might have to use Cocoa to corral him into a good decision."

Olivia laughed and waved, then scanned the field as Rachel took off back toward the house. She could see two men on horses, two standing, and beyond them, the herd. But with their distance from the truck, Olivia couldn't pick out Cash. Did Rachel have to drive off so fast? Olivia suddenly felt very alone.

She shook off the fear and strode toward the ranch truck. Cash had once thought her worth waiting for, and now she needed to prove he was worth fighting for. At the open tailgate, Olivia pulled herself up, then stood in the bed of the truck, using her hand to shade the sun. Still no way to recognize the man she wanted for her future husband.

She cupped hands around her mouth, ignored her racing heartbeat and yelled at the highest volume she could muster, "Cash Maddox!"

Four cowboy hats turned toward her. Olivia's stomach seemed to bounce along the metal truck bed when one man and horse pulled away from the group and came in her direction. Cash's green-and-gray plaid shirtsleeves were rolled up, and his tanned arms flexed when he pulled the horse to a stop by the bed of the truck.

When he started to dismount, Olivia held up a hand. "Stay there. I have something to say."

Cash responded with a slow head nod. Oh, man. What had she planned to say? All the words disappeared, leaving her chest fluttering.

After one steadying breath, she jumped in. "I shouldn't have lied to you. At first I didn't mean to, but then…" Tears? Seriously? She'd planned to be so strong during this speech. Olivia ignored the moisture slipping down her cheeks. "Then I lied because I was afraid. And it hurt so much to talk about it. I didn't want anyone to know. I thought if I kept everything hidden, that I could start over in Texas without all of that pain. Turns out, that's not how it works. The guilt and shame just followed me. I've finally figured out how to move on. I've finally forgiven myself."

Cash shifted on his horse but didn't speak.

"And I'm so sorry for not telling you the truth. I really hope you can forgive me, because—" Olivia paused, wishing for armor in case a rejection followed her words. She might be David facing Goliath, but she could do this. It was real this time. God approved. Only instead of five stones, she had three words. "I love you."

Cash slid down from the horse and put one boot on the bumper, pulling himself up into the truck bed with her. He paused a foot away, looking larger than life. Close, but still not quite attainable. "Are you done?"

Olivia pressed her lips together and nodded.

"Will you forgive me for what I said, for how I responded that night?"

Hope rose up. "I already have."

One stride brought him to her. He buried fingers in her hair, studying her face with such raw emotion that chills erupted across her skin. "I love you, too." In the next moment, his lips met hers, filled with a stunning mix of need and apology. She melted at the message, feeling the last vestiges of hurt release. The kiss wrapped her in forgiveness, in grace, in the future. When cheers and whistles sounded from the ranch hands, Cash's lips left hers to share a smile. He lifted his hat and waved it over his head in response to the guys, his gaze never leaving hers.

He thumbed the moisture from her cheeks. "I'm sorry for not letting anything go, for not trusting you. Even though you hid it, I know your real heart. And you are *nothing* like Tera."

The air rushed from her lungs. "It's about time you figured that out."

His lips traced across her damp cheeks and found her mouth again, distracting them from conversation for a minute. He broke the kiss to the sound of a few more whistles and someone calling out, "'Bout time!"

Olivia laughed and winced. "I'm sorry if I embarrassed you in front of the guys."

Humor danced in his eyes. "You can embarrass me anytime you want. Weren't you supposed to fly back tomorrow?"

She squinted at him. "Yeah. My flight was canceled over break and I had to reschedule. Why?"

"I planned to ask Janie to stay home so that I could pick you up at the airport. I had a few things to say to you." The slow curve of his lips made her legs turn to liquid. He tucked a piece of hair behind her ear, mischievous smile growing. "But now you said *I love you* first."

Olivia groaned. "That's going to be our thing, isn't it? That I said it first?"

"Yep." Cash scooped her up in a hug that made her feet fly off the truck bed. "You're going to have to live with that forever."

Forever. Olivia's arms wrapped around his neck. "Deal."

Epilogue

Olivia grabbed her bag of papers to grade and headed for the school parking lot. The March sun shone down, and despite the fact that she planned to catch up on grading during spring break, she couldn't help the smile on her face…especially when she noticed Cash leaning against his boat attached to his truck in the school parking lot.

She approached, using a hand to shade against the sun. "Going somewhere?"

Cash's arms were crisscrossed against his black Henley shirt, his grin growing with each step she took. "Just hoping to take a beautiful girl fishing."

"Don't you have to work?"

"I'm taking the day off."

"Spending the day with you I'm sure about. But fishing?" Her nose wrinkled, shoulders lifting. "I might have to be convinced."

With a slow grin, Cash reached out, fisting the

sides of the sweatshirt she wore open over a white V-neck T-shirt, tugging her forward until her flip-flops met his tennis shoes and his lips found hers.

She would crash into this man any day.

When he broke the kiss and stepped back, Olivia swayed, then righted her balance. "Okay." Her lips curved. "I'm in."

Cash opened the passenger door to his truck. "Your chariot awaits."

Olivia put her things into the backseat. The drive to the lake was peaceful, beautiful and filled with one of her favorite things—the man next to her. Soon, Cash backed the boat into the water and they flew across the lake. Olivia gathered her wind-blown hair and held it in a twist at the back of her neck until he slowed and put the anchor down.

He grabbed the fishing poles and handed her one. It took the man less than a minute to get his line baited and cork floating on the surface of the water.

Olivia slipped out of her sweatshirt, nibbling on her lip as she tried to bait the hook.

"Need some help, city girl? I'll do it for you." Cash's amused tone wasn't helping anything.

"No. I'll do it myself." Slimy thing.

"You could use one of the lures in the tackle box. Check it out and see if that would be easier to use as bait instead of the worm."

"I can do it."

"Could you grab the red lure out of the tackle box, then? I'm thinking about switching. The fish aren't biting on the worms."

Olivia borrowed a Rachel-sized huff and tossed the worm back into the can. Couldn't the man get the lure himself? She wiped her dirty hand on her jeans and reached for the tackle box, noticing a cooler in the boat. Had Cash packed a picnic? The day was getting better. And if that cooler contained chocolate, then the fishing might be worth it.

Four drawers opened on either side as Olivia pulled the tackle box open. Lures of every color, shape and size competed for space. But the small black velvet jewelry box? That was a new addition.

Cash made his way down to her end of the boat and took the seat across from her. "Open it."

She picked it up and slowly flipped back the lid. Nestled inside was a platinum diamond ring that glimmered in the sunshine.

Olivia glanced up to see Cash leaning forward.

"It was my mom's. And I really want it to be yours."

She opened her mouth to answer, but Cash tugged her forward until only inches separated them. "Now just hold on. I'm not done asking."

His hands slid along her arms, settling at her wrists. Could he feel her fluttering pulse? "Liv Grayson, thank you for being the first to say *I love you*—" Olivia squeaked in protest and Cash's chest shook with quiet laughter before he continued. "For being my sister's confidante and mentor, and the love of my life. Will you marry me?"

"Are you done ask—" A firm kiss stopped her sassy reply.

"Answer the question, woman."

"Yes." Definitely yes.

Cash slipped the ring on her finger, and she sucked in a breath as she studied the new addition.

It fit.

"How did you get it sized already?"

"I didn't. I thought we could do it after. But I should have known we wouldn't need to. You're perfect for me. Why wouldn't the ring fit?"

Cash lifted her hand, kissing the back of the ring and her finger. "I wish my parents could be here to meet you. But I know they know. They always prayed for my future wife, even when I was young and thought marriage and girls were gross. Although now I have a slightly different opinion about marriage."

Olivia laughed, fighting a surge of emotions at the same time. "You know, I think those prayers lived on even when they didn't, because it definitely took some prayer to get the two of us together."

"I've never thought of it that way, but I'm sure you're right. Which, if I understand marriage correctly, is something I need to plan to say a lot over the next…fifty years or so."

"Sounds good to me."

He laughed, tucking a strand of wind-loosened hair behind her ear. "I'm thinking we elope. France?"

"I'd marry you in a barn with Cocoa as the ring bearer."

"Now that sounds like a good idea. Although getting married in the back of a truck seems more fitting with our relationship."

Olivia laughed. "I can picture it now. What did I start?"

"Us." His lips met hers as his hands threaded through her hair, that simple soap smell he sported filling her senses. Images of the future flashed through her mind—children running through the ranch house, Aunt Rachel teaching them the art of stubborn, Janie and Jack as surrogate aunt and uncle, lots of hard work, love and laughter.

Olivia sighed when the kiss ended. "You are seriously brilliant, buckaroo."

"Why?" Cash narrowed his eyes, though the laugh lines at the corners crinkled. "Because I asked you to marry me?"

"Well, that, too. But also because you proposed while fishing. Which I now like infinitely better than I did ten minutes ago."

Cash's laugh echoed off the water. "I might have

to agree with you." His arms tightened around her. "Because you are definitely the best thing I've ever caught while fishing."

* * * * *

Dear Reader,

A question lies at the heart of this book: Does God use everything in our lives—even our mistakes—for His glory?

Before I became a stay-at-home mom, I worked at a crisis pregnancy center. Over and over, the issues of shame, guilt and regret played out before me—from women suffering decades after an abortion to teenagers being lied to by our culture, leaving them confused and longing for the truth. Jesus is the truth, and His truth is grace. Everyone has their own story, but the freedom and forgiveness remain the same.

Olivia believes her past isn't redeemable, but God ultimately uses it to rescue a teenager from making the same mistake. The most beautiful part of any redemption story is the grace God freely gives. We cannot earn it. It's a gift without strings, simply there waiting for us.

I'd love to connect with you. I'm on Facebook and Twitter as Jill Lynn Author, or stop by my website: www.Jill-Lynn.com.

Jill Lynn

LARGER-PRINT BOOKS!

GET 2 FREE
LARGER-PRINT NOVELS
PLUS 2 FREE
MYSTERY GIFTS

Love Inspired®
SUSPENSE
RIVETING INSPIRATIONAL ROMANCE

Larger-print novels are now available...

LISLPDIR13R

ReaderService.com

Manage your account online!

- Review your order history
- Manage your payments
- Update your address

> ### *We've designed the Harlequin® Reader Service website just for you.*

Enjoy all the features!

- Reader excerpts from any series
- Respond to mailings and special monthly offers
- Discover new series available to you
- Browse the Bonus Bucks catalog
- Share your feedback

Visit us at:
ReaderService.com